The Blessing Bowl

San Daniel

Published by San Daniel, 2022.

THE BLESSING BOWL

First edition. January 25, 2022.

Copyright © 2022 San Daniel.

ISBN: 979-8201088101

Written by San Daniel.

The Blessing Bowl

I had been in Canada again for a few months and winter was approaching fast. It had become cold and it snowed slightly. It was drifting snow and a light layer formed on the sidewalk in front of our house. You have that in the prairie states it snows almost daily in the cold months and the temperature yo-yos back and forth from plus 5 to -20 only to then slowly rise again in a repetitive cycle.

"Chinooks from Montana do that," my neighbor had explained to me. I did not want to ask what a Chinook exactly was but I had nodded wisely and I had started clearing snow again. Once inside, I immediately searched the internet for Chinook and then I learned that temperature fluctuations of 20 to 30 degrees Celsius were not rare.

I looked into the back garden and saw how everything had turned white. Occasionally I took a sip of tea from my mug and I felt satisfied. There was a knock at the door and that surprised me because I didn't expect anyone.

When I opened the door I saw in the light of my outdoor lamp that two elderly women were standing in front of my door. The right-most figure had something in her hands that she held out. They looked poorly dressed. "They are begging," I thought, "for some good cause or for the Salvation army or something."

It started snowing harder and a gust of cold wind made me shiver. "Ladies," I asked, "what can I do for you," and my hand went to my wallet.

"We are here," the woman on the left said to the person standing on the right and holding out a bowl in front of her. "What a hideous thing," subconsciously went through me, "I would never buy something like that." It started to snow harder now and I could hardly distinguish the street beyond the ladies.

"It's yours," said the right woman, "we've come to bring it." She now held out her two hands. The next gust of wind made me shiver, " why don't you come in, I suggested," then we'll talk further.

They stepped past me and I closed the door. "Would you like some tea," I asked as I walked to the table, "I just made a minute ago." There was no answer, but the woman with the dish placed it on the table and the other one pulled two chairs closer.

In my student days I had once something like this happening to me with 2 Jehovah's witnesses, whom I had invited in from the pouring rain to take shelter. I had just been peeling an apple when they rang the bell and I felt sorry for them. "Come in," I had said, and I had offered a slice of apple. "But we'll agree we are not going to talk about your faith, because I have no need for it."

The water had dripped from their long coats and they had sat down on the only couch that I was rich, while I sat down on the bed. It had gone wrong, the oldest man had opened a green Bible with underlined texts and thanked me for letting him in. It took 10 minutes before I had worked them out of the house as civilized as possible.

I had vowed that I would never allow something like that in my life anymore and there I was sitting at my breakfast table with three mugs of tea and two ladies that I probably shouldn't have let in.

The one woman who had carried the bowl was dressed entirely in black and had placed the it in front of her, she had a discomforting appearance. "This is a gift," she said in a flat tone, "that cannot be refused." I once took a sip of tea. "May I know," I asked, "why you are bringing me a present and what is it?" The Spirit ordered me, "she said as if that explained everything.

"The spirit," I repeated questioningly. "Yes," said the woman, "he always tells me what to do." The second woman now put down her cup, "It's a blessing," she said as if everything was clear now. "A what," I asked? "A blessing bowl," she repeated articulating it slowly. "Right," I said, and I realized that I had never heard of such a thing.

It remained silent for a moment and we drank some tea and I looked at the bowl that seemed quite unpleasant and unattractive. I would look it up later on the internet, I thought.

To break the silence, I picked up the thread again. "Thanks," I said, "I didn't expect this." "Nobody expects the bowl to be brought," the woman with the bad appearance said emphatically. "I can picture that," I laughed. "It's more the place," the second woman added. "You only just moved in, but the house is where the bowl belongs." I was indeed not the first owner. My house was old, it was built in 1901 and in Canada that is very old.

"It's not all clear to me," I reported, "but I do have some questions, That Spirit is that a person or who is it all about." You are sitting here with the Spirit, "said the woman with a tone of impatience. "What do you mean," I asked, feeling a slight shudder. "He is always next to me and tells me what to do, we are on a mission."

"Now he's standing next to you," I asked, and it had unintentionally had a tone of disbelief. "*Here*," she said, pointing to the spot between the two ladies.

"Goodness," I thought, "I'm sitting at the table with two crazy ladies, stay calm ... drink your tea quietly and then 'bonjour' them away nicely."

"It tires her out," said the second woman, "she prays 6 hours a day, but if the Holy Spirit demands it, she'll pray longer." The woman with the sinister look agreed, "it sucks all my energy away. But yes, he works through me and that increases his reach. "

Had it been my imagination or had I not noticed the lightfall in the bowl before? I turned away. "That's quite something," I said, thinking by myself "humor the fools, they'll be gone soon, their tea will be gone and they will disappear into the street and out of my life." I put down my mug and continued, "I must say that I do not see the Spirit, as it were, but that does not mean everything."

"He who doubts the Spirit," said the woman seriously, "is lost." "Tell him about your clothes and stuff," said the second woman, and he'll get it, "and she looked at me penetratingly. "She is the tool, the voice that speaks, repeats what no one hears." "They are crazy," I thought, "probably not dangerous, but as crazy as they come."

"I am listening," I said, as strange as it was, it fascinated me. "Before I go to church," the woman with the dark gaze said, "I put down some items of clothing and the Spirit tells me what to wear and then I know which church to attend."

"I don't follow you completely," I said, "what does that dress have to do with the church." If I have to wear flat shoes, that means that I have to go to the church of the Salvation Army, they are poor buggers, you cannot come in high heels, that would make them envious or it would insult them.

'Dark clothing is more for the Lutheran church they are not frivolous. In the Catholic Church I can put on anything I want, it doesn't matter. Sometimes the Spirit teases me and then I wear clothes and then when I am on my way to the matching church, he forces me to cross the street and I finally arrive at a completely different church, that is a test of whether I am obedient enough. "

"You didn't know me," I said slowly, "but have you followed your inner voice to my door?" "Yes," the second woman exclaimed! "This is the place and you are the chosen one and now you have the symbol of the connection." I wanted to know more, but the woman in black started talking to the sky. "I'm sorry, Lord, we're going right away," and she got up in a hurry.

The mugs were put down and with a few steps they were at the door, which was pulled shut behind them, and without saying another word, leaving me behind in astonishment, they had disappeared. Only the mugs on the table and the bowl on the table testified of their previous presence.

I looked again at the bowl, "I'll leave it where it was placed," I resolved, and I had never been superstitious, but the bowl gave me a feeling of revulsion, and deep in my heart I knew I never wanted to touch it.

"Schizophrenics, they must have been, I thought, but would two schizophrenics find each other and then have a common delusion," I did not know and decided to consult my PC about these matters.

My life's companion returned from the coffee in the village and looked in amazement at the bowl on the table. You couldn't fail but notice it. Dark colors and hideous in shape. "What is that," she wanted to know, "where did you get that?" "I've had a visit," I replied, "a strange visit." In the meantime, I cleaned up the mugs and put them in the sink. "If you fancy another cup of coffee," I inquired, "I can tell you how it came about."

A little later we were seated with a cup of comfort, and when I was done, my wife said, "you let anyone in now, don't you?" "Yes and no," I said, it actually sort of happened to me, and it all didn't sound so strange when I summarized it, like: "Two ladies came by and they left a bowl, but in reality it was very oppressive and I was happy when they left. "

My wife once looked intently at the bowl, "it is downright ugly," she concluded, "" but that's not the point, I think it's bad, ominous. " My wife had put it well into words, "ominous," that pretty much described the feeling I had when the bowl was brought to my house. The woman in the dark dress had made me feel disturbed with her Spirit gibberish.

"Hmm," she said, "I have never heard of such a bowl, I will ask a friend of mine, who is from here and knows more about the habits that apparently apply here.

I stared a bit lost in front of me and saw how my wife was busy typing on her tablet. My eye was involuntarily drawn to the bowl and for a moment I thought I saw another light fall, but when I looked more closely I saw that I was mistaken, the bowl was just dark and dark. The early twilight had fallen and no light from outside could have possibly entered through the window, "imagination," I soothed my perception.

Moments later the well-known Apple tune sounded that announced a message. " That will be Anja," my wife said triumphantly, "let's see what she has to say." "I didn't think so, you see," my wife said, "something like that has not happened here at all and she has no idea what such a bowl is or what it looks like."

"Take a picture of it," I suggested, "and send it to her, then she will have a better idea of what that bowl looks like." Two flashes lit up the thing and my wife typed in some text. "This is the one," she read, "a photo from above and one from the side."

A gust of wind flicked a branch against the window and gave me a frighten. "Draw the curtains please," my wife asked, "the wind is on the rise," and she tapped enter. I stood frozen, the light went out and on, and then stayed out, and then came on again. "It will be heavy weather," I said, "I thought we had lost the light." "We've lost the internet," my dearest reported.'

Her tablet had a red exclamation mark behind the photos with the text: not sent, typical Apple, I thought, "not just an exclamation mark, no a red exclamation mark."

The familiar tune sounded again and my wife read the message that appeared on screen. "It is Anja," she reported, "she has received the text but not the photos." "Hey," I cried, "I thought the internet was down." "It is", my wife said, weighing every word, "but the exclamation mark is still behind the photos."

I looked at my cell phone and saw that I had internet and suddenly I had enough of weird women who came to my door with bowls and dragging a

Spirit in their wake. "Come on," I said, 'we'll go to the living room and watch something from Netflix. "That's not possible," my beloved said, "the internet is down," and she looked confused at me. "We'll take a look," I suggested, "it can't hurt."

The screen clicked on while my wife had put her croche on her lap, two glasses of wine were waiting for us at the side table. "This not too bad," I laughed, "we have internet again."

The feeling of oppression had diminished, I realized and I knew how it came but did not want to say it, I was further away from the bowl, that caused it. I did not want to admit it, but I knew in my soul that it was the case.

I pushed the feeling away, but the fact that I knew where that bowl was dominated my thinking. "Come on," I exhorted myself, "you're not superstitious." But the rational voice in my head was silenced by a core thought, "I wish I hadn't been home when those women came by.

The episodes that followed were a documentary about Alaska's untouched beauty, the last frontier that could still be explored. It was a wild landscape with forests and canyons, mountains that were touching heaven, with caverns and caves where you could expect bears, with a valley through which a wild river twisted.

"Sweety," I said after a while, "I'll just turn in because tomorrow my sister will come by early and we will go to Saskatoon and that is a long drive and it is snowing and you never know what the road condition will be like. " "I'll be right there," she replied, "just warm my bed up .."

As I walked past the table my eye was drawn to the bowl and I forced myself to take my gaze away from the urn, I confessed it to myself, no doubt, the bowl was scary. With large steps, bigger than I wanted, I quickly walked past the table and on to the bedroom and a moment later I was in bed.

I woke up when my love came in and sat up in bed. "It's me," she said in a low voice, "go back to sleep." For a moment I thought that the dark woman had entered my room, ridiculous thought, but if you are awakened roughly from your sleep, the brain still works with images and symbols from the dream world and it takes a while before reality, the form of reality as we know it, returns.

I fell into a deep sleep and found myself in a wild landscape. In the distance, mountains towered and the sky was crispy fresh. I was walking across a plain and felt unprotected, occasionally there was a tree but I walked into desolation and felt lost and lonely. The sky was overcast and it was quickly darkening and a gust of wind touched the grass. I just had the idea that it had to do with me and felt uncomfortable as if I was being spied upon.

But the plain was endless and I didn't know how I got there nor why I walked there. I would see the person who was looking at me, if such a person was present but I did not see anyone because no one was there. Still, the feeling came over me that I was being watched.

Where I walked everything seemed sterile, there was no other life to be found than the grass with the occasional tree and then the endless plain again. I had to go to the mountains and I can only say that they attracted me. How did I end up in that area and what was my purpose? "I'm searching," I thought, "and I don't know where I am because I didn't have a starting point." That seemed like a truth to me, a revelation and I let it sink in, what was the reason for my existence and what was my ultimate goal?

"I had gone lost during my journey," I realized, "but when had that happened?" The answer was already planted in my head. "*You always gradually lose yourself on your journey*, it does not happen overnight, it is a growth process, sometimes you just do not arrive." Meanwhile, the mountains came closer and it gave me a sense of security, I had been so unprotected on the plain, I longed for the safety of being hidden.

I turned and tossed in my bed and fell a sleep again.

Now I stood under the mountain that turned me into a dwarf and decided to follow the path up. The sky had turned black and a lightning bolt cleaved through the sky and hit a tree behind me. I heard the blow almost simultaneously while seeing the flash. The tree smoked and was split to the ground. " Good that I was off the plain, "I thought, until a second impact followed. I jumped up in shock, my heart thumped in my throat and my ears ached. I smelt the strong release of ozone.

When the third impact hit the ground to the right of me and the ground crashed and trembled under my feet and was followed by an impact to my left and I was knocked over by the force of the impact, I scrambled up and started running. "I am being hunted, I am being sought and found," it flashed through me, "run for your life," was the only thing that came to mind ... and I ran, followed by an impact here, which threw stones up and an impact there, which flamed across the ground.

I had become a deer, I ran without purpose, I ran to run and I was driven on, and I did not look where I was going, I just ran, I had become a pair of lungs, swallowing howling breaths, and a pair of legs that rushed on.

In the distance I saw an overhanging cliff with an opening in it, a cave and at full speed I raced there. I almost dived into it. Hiding was the only thing I could do or I would be destroyed by the flashes that followed me. I did not realize that the cave was dimly lit. I ran inside, far from the opening and stumbled and landed hard on the stone surface, a blow that drove the last bit of air out of me.

So I lay there gasping for breath and slowly the awareness of my being came back, and I got up to see in horror what caused the faint glow. In front of me was an elevation that reflected a light fall from nowhere. It was a bowl, it was **the** dark bowl, and I knew that I was lost and would not achieve my goal, not now and never again, and I collapsed. "Oh my God," I thought, "there is a grail and there is a dark grail and this is **that** dark grail."

Someone was shaking me and plains, and the bolts and the cave and the diabolical bowl fell off me, while I floated upward from the dreams that had weighed me down. "It's time," said the voice, "would you like some coffee, your sister will be here soon." I muttered something that sounded like "yes," and the images of the cave still filled the space that was my bedroom. I felt with my hand above my head and found the light switch and the cave became my own house.

The first thing I saw when I walked into the kitchen was the table with the bowl and I knew that the bowl had dominated my night. The coffee was steaming and I took a sip and washed the bitter coffee around my mouth. "Thank you," I said, "I needed that, you don't want to know what a bad dream I had." "You have kept me awake," my wife said, "you were tossing and turning and you screamed occasionally."

When I wanted to tell what I dreamed, my words were just fragments of a fabric that would exist for a while and then would disappear. They did not cover the load. "I was alone," I began, "and lonely and lost, and I didn't know where I was or what to do." It sounded innocent, but I had walked and run in a world, and had been haunted by diabolical lightning. Words did not describe what I had seen or felt and I left it at that.

"Did you sleep well," I just asked to say something. "No," the love of my life replied, I was swimming in a lake and was drawn to the center by a light current. No one was there, and the sky was overcast, I felt very alone. When I wanted to swim to the shore again, the current became stronger and without a doubt I was drawn to the middle of the lake. The sky became pitch black and I wanted to get to the shore but the bank moved away from me per second.

It started to hail and circles splashed around me, and I was obscured by the curtain of splashing water and hail, so that if anyone had been on the beach, they would not have seen me.

This was strange, and just as I was wondering what was taking me so far, out of sight of the shore and worried if it would be a whirlpool, a shadow came, a silhouette, gliding lightly across the water.

The shadow was an old rowing boat without oars and it came towards me, attracted by the same current. "If I only can get in there," I thought, my wife said. "As it got closer, however, I just wanted to get as far away as possible from the boat." Oh, "I said in surprise when I had swallowed a sip of coffee," but you wanted to scramble on board? " My wife looked at me. "No," she said, "there was something placed on the bow ..." and she kept her mouth shut and looked at the bowl that was still in the same place where the women had put it.

"And," I asked? "Fortunately, you woke me up," she said, "you seemed to have been thrown against me and you were gasping so much that I thought you were having a heart attack." I didn't want to ask, but I thought I knew what had been on that bow. Our dream consultation ended because there was a knock at the door and my sister came in.

"Good morning," she said, "not for nothing, but you have to keep your door locked at night." I nodded but I knew with great certainty that I had done just that, it was the last thing I always did before I went to sleep, checking the door, just as routine like as brushing your teeth.

"Come on," she said, "we're going to Saskatoon, the roads are snow-free and I'm looking forward to it." Five minutes later, her Dodge drove away from my house, my love waved us goodbye. We would drive 400 kilometers, have lunch with my nephew and then drive back the 400 kilometers. It was going to be a long day.

It was still dark when we left the village and we were both immersed in our own thoughts. I found it striking that the bowl had also appeared in my loved one's dream. Two out of two is good statistics and I knew that to be very unlikely from my earlier studies. All the events that cast shadows ahead in our lives and turned them into symbols in our sleep were variables within variables.

In both cases there had been a threat and the presence of the pagan bowl. In both cases the threat had consisted of powers of nature, in my case lightning that wanted to destroy me and it had been a current with my love, drawing her away from the coastline. In both cases we had experienced a deep sense of abandonment. Those would have been the similarities, and I thought again how unlikely it would be if we experienced these happenings in a dream world together in the same house at the same time. I understood what had happened and it made me shudder it had been images that had been sent or that had been influenced by the presence of the evil that had been set down in my house.

Arriving on the main road, I started my story about the two women who had appeared at my door. I didn't like that word: appeared, but I realized that I experienced it that way. Unknowingly we make word choices that betray our deeper feelings, and probably those chosen words are driven by an instinct that defends our own protection.

"I'm listening," my sister said, "you seemed absent for a moment." I picked up the thread again and told aboout the Jehovah's in my student days and how I had let them come in because it was raining as I had felt compassion. Eventually I arrived at the bowl, the blessing bowl.

"I have never heard of such a thing," my sister said, who had listened very carefully to the story. She could listen well, she had worked as a social worker / psychologist until she retired and saw through people in a flash and could listen well. "No," she repeated, "never!"

When I also spoke about the allegation of the Spirit who always sat or stood next to the woman and told her where she was going, she gave me a sideways look.

"I don't like that," she said decisively, "schizophrenia occurs of course and people might think they hear voices. Nor is compulsive action unknown to me. I have had patients who always wanted to walk in the gutter with one foot on the street and with the other on the sidewalk. Or were never 'allowed' to step on joints between tiles or climb stairs two at a time or always gave a light tap to every second lamppost in passing. Those are compulsive neuroses. I have also experienced those that suffer from religious insanities but they are all different syndromes with different backgrounds. '

I could picture that and nodded. "You will not soon see a cluster of syndromes that are intertwined and connected for underlying reasons," my sister said earnestly. 'Nor will such a thing be accompanied by gifts that are given or brought, no matter how positive or negative. It sounds more like a mission, self-imposed or "ordered," or the fulfillment of a promise or obligation. "

"It sounds serious," she continued, "it gives me an indefinable feeling when I let my instincts speak. Apparently the bowl had to do with the location rather than with the person staying there, you said that yourself. Although you are now connected to that bowl and so is your partner, because you are staying at that location."

That was a razor-sharp analysis expressed by my sister," I thought. My sister had always been deeply religious and had been on the brink of studying theology. She was very analytical and contemplative in nature and I attached great importance to her opinions. "Then how would you explain it," I asked? "Ten people, ten opinions," she smiled, "but I'm worried about that bowl and for a clear reason."

"I'm listening," I said simply. "If that woman with the gloomy appearance claimed that the Spirit was draining her energy," my sister continued, "I can tell you that she thinks she has the Spirit next to her, but such is not the case. On the contrary, the Holy Spirit gives people hope and energy and does not suck the energy away from the elected ones, it would make them victims rather than saved sinners. "Oh dear," I thought, 'here comes the church talk', but I listened carefully because I realized that my sister was right ... at least from a philosophical point of view.

"What then," I asked because I was curious what she would think of it. "Something bad, something demonic," my sister simply said away. Not only are the people bringing the bowl under the influence of what they think is the Spirit who directs them, but they let themselves be misled by something bad and let themselves be used as tools. That is obedience a bit like a form of worship in a submissive relationship with what they believe drives them. "

"Let's assume for the time being something like that is possible," I suggested, "are those women dangerous." "They are just the messengers," my sister suggested, "the helpers of something that reaches out to you and your house and everyone who is there." "What do you base such a thing on," I wanted to know? "On the Bible," said my sister, who could just as easily have become a pastor or priest. "Because ...," I made it sound like a question. "Because the Bible does not support something like a blessing bowl," my sister spoke as if she had just explained a difficult sum to a dull boy.

"Wait a minute, the Bible was recorded thousands of years ago," I objected, "and time has not stood still." The moon landing and the Apolo astonauts, for example, do not appear in the Bible either, but it did happen and it did take place. "

"In the Bible," my sister said emphatically, "there is no such thing as a blessing bowl, but demons and curses and blessings, are and I'm talking about that." That bowl has nothing to do with whatever form of blessings. " Incidentally, curses and blessings go side by side. What is a blessing today is a curse tomorrow. " I didn't know exactly what to do with that and if the bowl hadn't bothered me so much, I would have enjoyed the word plays with my sister.

"Take a man who loves a woman with all his heart," said my sister, "and she falls for a lover, cheating on him, then jealousy strikes and the man will hate the woman forever." A gift that is not accepted has, after a while, become something ugly that only produces negativity. "

The Bible supports that, "I teased her? "Balaam, part II (Numbers 22: verses 36-24: 25)," she said, "there is almost no clearer case." "I understand every word you've just spoken but I don't know what you're saying," I explained. "Balaam and Balak king of the Moabites," my Bible-learned sister clarified. "Oh," my sister laughed, "come on then, Balak wanted to destroy the Israelites and had Balaam come to a battlefield to curse them." On the way to Balak, his mule refused to walk. He whipped his beast of burden, but the beast was terrified and did not move.

The beast felt what did not register with Balaam, a presence that would kill Balaam if he performed his mission. When Balak and Balaam oversaw the army of Israel, Balaam wanted to curse it but only blessings came from his mouth. "So far the reading," said my sister.

We had arrived in Saskatoon, talking and arguing, and had almost come to my nephew's house. I decided to continue discussing the bloody bowl on the return trip. When I looked above the apartment building I was shocked, for a moment I thought I had seen the silhouette of the bowl in the shape of a dark cloud, but when I blinked my eyes it was just a cloud again. "I have become obsessed," I thought, "but it had been the form, do not fool yourself," was my next thought, and I knew it to have been true and it had hung over my nephew's apartment.

My nephew had studied history and just bought a flat. "Great," I thought, "if you can start like that in your life." The greeting was warm and welcoming, we were very close, we enjoyed a common interest in the world and its current events and I gladly visited him. The distances are always great in North America and people don't really mind travelling the mile. I always had the idea that we in Europe have no idea of what distances mean and the North Americans have no idea of history. Canada is only 140 years old and it is difficult to explain that Amsterdam already had city rights in the year 900.

The flat was beautiful and after viewing it we all decided to go for a bite to eat at Fudd Ruckers .. and marketing wise I thought that was a clever chosen name,because many would remember it by reversing the first letters Rudd ... f ... I'm not so keen on burger joints but to be honest, this was a modern implementation of everything that is wrong with fast food. It wasn't bad with a salad bar that you could choose from and in short, I didn't eat bad at all.

My sister and I exchanged some pleasantries with my nephew and then she announced that she had to do some shopping and whether we'd liked to go to the *'fox and hound'* a typical gentleman's bar. There we would meet again, before driving the 4 hours back to our village.

There we sat behind our pint of 'Olson Canadian'. "Cheers," I said, raising the glass. "How is your new work," I asked to say something. "It takes some getting used to," my nephew replied, "but I like it."

"Nice," I replied, "I'm happy about that." We sat like that for a while and looked at a large screen where a hockey game was taking place. "Any special things in your life," I asked, almost interested? I meant meetings with female beauties or plans for the future.

"Hmm," he said, "I don't know, something weird has happened and I don't know if I should tell you or not?" "Come on," I said, "get it off your chest, who is the lucky lady?" "Well, it's about something else," my nephew said, who never kept any secret from me. "I am listening," I said, and I was, waiting for what was to come.

"Uncle San," my nephew began, "do you believe in supernatural events." "Hmm," I replied, "yes and no, I am not convinced new age, but I do think that inexplicable things sometimes happen, why?"

"Just before you came," my nephew said, "I experienced something that really got to me." "I am listening," was my standard answer. "What did you experience?" "I only tell you this if it stays here between us," my nephew explained. "You have my word," I said solemnly and took a sip of beer.

"I watched TV and waited for both of you," my nephew began, "and then I just heard a heavy irregular panting, I watched where it came from and it came from the easy chair next to me." A deep shiver ran down my spine, my poor nephew, I had seen the cloud, something like that has a reason.

I played innocent, "what do you mean a panting came from the seat next to you," I asked. My nephew looked uncomfortable, "the chair was slightly dented at the seat," he said, "as if something had taken its place and the panting sounded from there." Right, "I said," and what did you think? " "I couldn't think," my nephew replied, "I was frightened." "I would have been," I thought, but I said, "and what do you think it was?" "I don't know," my nephew almost moaned, "but It gave me almost got a heart attack, I was so scared, my heart was pounding in my ears." "Yes," I said, "and then what?" You rang the doorbell and it was as if a spell had been broken. "

"Exactly," I said, "that won't happen again, they are one-off events, believe me," and I thought, "it won't happen anymore because I won't be visiting you again from now on." I knew it, my presence had cast my shadow forward, the damned dish that was connected to me by those two nasty women had caused this. Our conversation stopped because my sister came in and cheerfully announced that we had to leave again.

My sister drove deftly through the busy traffic in Saskatoon and it wasn't long before the neighborhood where my nephew lived came into view again. "Would the cloud be there again," I wondered, "the cloud that had been shaped like a blessing bowl." I realized that clouds took on many forms, as a child I'd see all sorts in them. I knew that I was appeasing my feelings. The cloud had looked like the bowl and had hung close to his flat.

In addition, my nephew had been visited by an entity while he was just watching TV. At least I assumed that, he certainly did not make it up, his way of doubting wether he would share it or not with me, had been too authentic. Why would you come up with something like that, anyway? He had known absolutely nothing about the bowl of blessings, and it had been noon, not a twilight evening that would create shadows and made people vulnerable.

So we drove on in silence to the neighborhood, each of us with our own thoughts. My sister probably already taking leave of her son, for whom she had traveled 800 kilometers back and forth that day to have lunch with. My nephew had seen us for a moment and would return to his own young independent life the minute we'd leave the street and I, yes, I was worried about events of which I didn't know where they would lead. "Some neighbors of mine will go ice fishing," my nephew said, maybe you would like to come and see that? " "Another time," his mother said decidantly, "we still have to drive 400 kilometers back and I don't want to drive in the dark."

"No cloud to be seen," I thought, with a feeling of relief. "Not above the flat and nowhere in the area, not a single cloud." Then there would not be some appearance in a chair waiting for my nephew. Then the revelation presented itself, the revelation that almost made me cringe, when it hit me in all its intensity. I was already sitting next to my nephew! That cloud had to do with the blessing bowl, and therefore with me. I never panted, that didn't fit in the puzzle, but in my dream I had fallen out of breath in front of the bowl on the rocky cave bottom.

"Don't go swimming, boy," I warned my nephew who gave me uncomprehensive look as the car stopped. It was winter, who would go swimming now. I understood that it must have sounded strange and I immediately said, "Never mind, I was deep in thought." "Yes, of course," my nephew murmured, but he looked at me strangely. My sister embraced her son and I shook his hand and wished him good luck with his new job, and a little later we drove out of the

quarters leaving my nephew behind who would now be left alone in Saskatoon without relatives.

"Maybe that is for the better," it went through me, "if he had never met me, the dark, the ineffable would not have taken place in his house. Would whatever had been there be now with me?" I had no idea.

"You are very quiet," my sister broke the silence, "and what exactly did you mean by the swimming bit?" I could not answer her because I had given my nephew my word over a beer not to mention it. "Right," I said, to give it a spin, "I was thinking about my love's dream and how the current had dragged her, it made no sense." "Really," her voice now sounded sharp, "if you don't want to say it, that's okay, but don't take the mickey out of me." She had read me once again.

The hours went by and the only stop we made was in Rosetown to refuel. We recalled memories and laughed and talked about the hippie era that we both experienced in a different way. She started singing '*Monday, Monday*' from the mamas and papas .. and from a distant past the words came to the fore and I was genuinely happy to be right next to my sister and sang fragments along. It was music from the early 60s and it had withstood the test of time.

Time passed and with time the distance and she began singing a few words, and I recognized the chords. "Hey," I said, "I know what that is, it's called '*Spirit in the sky*', and it was, it was...," I hurt my brain, "it was by Norman Greenbaum's," I suddenly shouted, "*a Jesus Freak* ." It had been hip psychedelic music. "Ha," I laughed, "we grew our hair over our ears and wanted to change the world, which was reasonably successful to a certain extent. We were *hip* and those who did not participate and continued to follow the establishment, were *the squares* and you had the *Jesus Freaks*. Who shouted all the while, "Jesus loves you."

After some digging the words came up and when my sister sang 'going up to the Spirit in the sky' at full blast, I heard, just beside me, actually between the driver's seat and me, a voice, it was a raw voice as if spoken through gravel and that voice turned to me and said, "*I have returned!*"

I froze and my mouth closed. My sister completed the song and then looked at me. "Hey dude," she said, "you didn't sing along." Then she looked at me for a moment and looked again at the road. "Are you okay?" She wanted to know. 'You want to stop somewhere to have a bite to eat? You look like you've just seen a ghost. "Spirit in the sky," I muttered. Had I really heard the voice?

I didn't even have to wonder, I really had heard the voice. Was I going insane or had that voice been there? My sister had not heard it, but then again she had been bellowing the song. I decided that the voice had really been there and leaned away from the center of the car. I decided not to share my thoughts anymore, something unholy had come to sit next to me and I wondered if the bearer of that voice's had first sat in a chair in Saskatoon. "

We turned down the main road and approached my house, "thank you for a nice day," I said, "You want to come in." "I'd like that," she replied.

"Hi there," my wife shouted from the kitchen. 'Would you fancy some coffee? We fancied a bit of dark comfort. "I told her about the bowl," I told my love. "Yes," said my sister, "I have a bad feeling about it, you shouldn't keep it here." "Hmm," my sweety said, pouring the coffee, "I've already solved that." I looked questioningly at her and she continued, "You know I took pictures and they were not sent." My sister crossed herself. "Yes," I agreed, "I was there, only the text was sent and the lights went off and on."

My wife gazed at me with a funny look and said, "The latter may have been a coincidence, although I doubt it." "Because," I asked ..? "Because the neighbors have not had a power outage," my sweetheart replied, "I was having coffee with the neighbor and I asked her and she has been home all day and there was no power outage." "alright," I said, "and we live side by side and the power comes from the same line."

"That is impossible," said my sister, and then she put her hand to her mouth, when the truth sank in. "Put that thing away," she commanded!

"I came home again," my darling continued, "and thought that if the photos had been on my camera, they should also be in my cloud." I took a sip of coffee, and when I swallowed it, I asked, "and ..." "Only the text is in the cloud," my wife said, "and that really isn't possible." "No," I confirmed, "that is impossible." She showed her tablet and it contained only the text.

"What are you going to do about it," my sister asked. "I have already done something about it," my wife announced proudly, "I have picked up the bowl and thrown it in the garbage, and it was emptied half an hour later, as if it were meant to be like that, and that is the end of all misery." " "*Sure*" the gravel voice sounded from beside me, and I choked violently. After coughing and choking and coughing, I looked at the table cloth and thought, "Was that my inner voice or was that a voice?"

"I'm glad you did so," my sister announced. "You didn't break it now, did you." "No," my wife replied, "I just threw it in the trash." "Very well," my sister thought, "you never know what could have been released by destroying it."

"Maybe the effect will fade away," I thought, and that somehow calmed me down a bit.

"I'll just call Saskatoon to report that we have arrived safely," my sister said and took her last sip of coffee. "Hello, dear boy, yes, yes it is me," I heard my sister say a moment later. "We have arrived safely. I am just having coffee with your uncle." "Oh, how horrible," I heard after some silence, "Praise God that you were not there, what a disaster." She listened again and continued, "I'll call you back from home in a minute, try to stay calm."

"It's terrible," she said to no one in particular, "something terrible has happened," "So what happened," I asked, alamated. "His three neighbors, you know, the ones that went ice fishing," I nodded, "they sank through the ice and all three of them drowned." "Good God," I said, thinking, 'it is that cursed bowl and the mess it projects.' "I am going home," my sister announced, "while she got up," that poor boy is completely upset, I am going to talk to him quietly, oh my, he could have been one of them. " I closed the door behind her and felt guilty for no apparent reason.

"I'll go and get the trashcan inside," I announced, "before the kids start kicking it about." I walked through the back garden, which was relatively long. Our house was from 1901, from the early days of the village and all the plots from that time had been large. It was one of the few brick-built houses, I was told by the broker, because there had been a brickyard at the beginning of the village, which used the clay from the creek for its stones. "Your house will still be standing when wooden houses are blown over by the first hurricane to hit us 'had been his sales pitch.

Our house also had a basement at elevated height that ran underneath the entire house with an exit to a small space in the garden that was closed off by a heavy hatch. "That," the broker had said, "is or was the coal chute, coal was dumped through the hatch in the past and then you scooped it into the basement in the boiler, which has now become a new gas-fired installation."

I stepped out of the gate and walked over to my gray bin, where my neighbor was already moaning. "Good day," he said,'how are you, "we are doing it wrong, we have to put the containers out at the last minute." "I am fine, " I replied, 'how are you and what do you mean at the last minute?" "Filthy stinking Indians," growled the man who was known in the neighborhood as a true racist. 'They go through your garbage and take out the plastic bottles,' he pointed to the floor around the bin, 'and the garbage truck goes by automatically, it lifts the bin and empties it, there is no longer a swamper who picks up bits of junk. "

"They hand in those bottles for a deposit, I have no problem with that," he pointed to the ground again, "but they simply leave everything else that they get out and I can pick it up again." "Right," I said, "I'll think about it."

'I just chased away another Indian who got all the rubbish out of your container, "he continued. An alarm bell rang. "I hope he went for the bottles," I asked. "That as well," said the neighbor, "he had arms full of junk." "Good God, no," I thought. "I came out and shouted from afar that he had to get lost," my neighbor said, "but he kept digging, then I grabbed my gun out of the truck and that lazy feather-ass ran off."

"Fine spoke man, my neighbor," went through me. I stooped and picked up some papers and threw them in my empty bin. "Thanks for the advice," I said, and I went back into my backyard to put the container behind my house. "Has it been emptied," my wife wanted to know when I came in. " "Certainly," I replied, "there was nothing left in it." "Nice," she said, "that sorts it out, I felt a bit threatened," and I knew what she meant.

A few minutes later we were sat rather cozy in the small lounge and watched Netflix with a glass of wine in front of us at a side table. "I'm glad the thing's gone," my dear said, and I agreed with her. I did wonder if I would still have the connection, for the bowl had been brought to the house and I lived there, would the connection have to do with distance, it had been given to me and I had more or less rejected it, my wife had thrown it away, but I would have agreed.

"Ridiculous," my normal inner voice went through me, "you are almost starting to believe that crap." I took a sip of wine and then the gravel voice rang out beside me. "*not **soooo** ridiculous, at all!*" I stiffened up and choked again. "Don't drink so eagerly," my wife admonished me, "you'll stay in it, first you choke on coffee and now on wine." I kept to myself why I had choked.

I felt relieved that the bowl had left our house and I sat relaxed next to my wife with a glass of wine, watching a documentary. It had been a long and eventful day and I was more tired than I wanted to admit. When my eyes closed occasionally, I leaned sideways and planted a kiss on my wife's cheek. "I should go to sleep," I announced, "my eyes keep falling shut and I want to get up early tomorrow." "Go and warm my bed up," my dear said, and a moment later I got up to check if the frontdoor was on the night lock.

It was and after a tooth-brushing ritual I rolled into my bed. I thought of my poor nephew who was confronted with three drowned neighbor boys and the long drive back that had been accompanied by theological and philosophical discussions. Just before falling asleep the garbage bin came into view with my neighbor who had complained about Indians taking all sorts out of the bins.

I slipped into the darkness and my consciousness left me. Then the images appeared and I knew where I was standing, for unclear reason I had ended up in my basement. I heard a soft thumping and just as I pointed my ears it stopped. "I shouldn't have gone downstairs," I thought, "basement hatches should remain closed when you go to sleep, what in God's name was I doing in my basement." I looked at where the stairs should be, but there were none. I looked up where the stairs should have been if I could see the cellar hatch, but the beams were uninterrupted.

The pounding began again, now a little louder and I saw the faint glow at the end of the basement. Something breathed deeply in and out behind me and my heart froze, it made me take a few steps forward. "Don't look back," I thought, "otherwise it will appear." It was a nonsensical thought, but I knew it to be the truth. "If you admit that something exists, you give it shape." *"It won't save you,"* the gravel voice sounded, followed by a mocking laughter, and I forced myself not to listen. "I am conjuring that up," I thought, "it's not there, I need to go back to bed."

The light blue glow came from around the corner from where my workplace was. "Oh my goodness," I thought, "that workshop is almost under the back terrace where the garbage cans are and that's where the light comes from. There was a pounding again, but now clearer, a heavy pounding and a breaking noise. "It doesn't just happen," I realized, "it is unholy what's there, something that wants to reach out like a hand of evil trying to find its way through the dark night and destroy whatever possible."

It was, it was ... and I knew it ... it was like walking up a staircase and you were afraid that something would grab you by your ankles or the monster in the closet or the evil lurking under your bed or sounds in the attic that you only could hear and all the fears of childhood took shape and now I felt the breathing in my neck and with stiff legs I took a few more steps forward.

The pounding became rhythmic and I heard voices, a murmur of voices and I knew that I had to walk on and the sweat beaded on my forehead. The walls seemed to deform and I felt heavy and I was drawn to my workshop, with knees trembling and a heart thumping in my throat, "save me," I begged almost loudly, "my basement looked like the cave and I knew what would be on the workbench in my workshop. "

The blow had been unbelievably harsh and came crashing down from above my head, and I sat up in my bed with a pajama still clinging to me with the sweat of fear and I heard a scraping sound as if something was sliding down our roof and then a loud blow to the back wall of our house. Then it was quiet. I turned on the light and my wife grabbed my arm, "what in God's name was that," she wanted to know, the horror had sounded through her voice. "I don't know," I said, "but we'll see tomorrow." We remained motionless and finally fell into a deep sleep again.

In the morning I put on some clothes and walked to the back garden to have a look at my roof. At least that was my intention, but I was stopped by large branches that I had to wriggle around, and those branches were attached to a large uprooted tree that ran through my neighbor's fence against my house.

Sticking from in between the shingles on my roof I saw smaller broken branches. That tree had first slowly, creaking in the wind, landed on my sloping roof and then slid off and hit the back of my house. The roof looked undamaged, but the colossus had thrown itself through the internet cable. "Better go see the neighbor," I resolved. It took a while for the door to open and there was a sleepy neighbor with his morning coat on.

"Good morning," he greeted me, "what can I do for you?" "Good morning," I greeted him back, "although we could leave the good out, a tree of yours has crossed our fence and ended up in our garden sliding down my roof." "I'm insured," he announced, "at Brightman's, I'll report it later to them." "I'll go by," I offered, "I have my insurance with them as well." "Okay, just let me know the outcome," he answered me and closed the door on me.

At Brightman's I had to wait for an old man who was chatting about anything and everything and then touched his hat in a salute and left the office.

"What can I do for you," asked the young man who was Brightman's son. "A tree from my neighbor was blown over and entered my garden passing my roof," I explained. "Injuries, damages," he asked with interest. "Just the fence," I answered. "Well then, that's settled," said the young man. "What do you mean it is settled," I wanted to know. "You take the tree away and you and your neighbor fix your fence," he said with a friendly smile.

"Who takes the tree away," I asked in surprise. "You, of course," said the young Brightman, it is your garden and what lies there is yours, or you leave the tree or you take it away. " "Why am I still insured," I asked in astonishment? "This is an act of God, so force majeure," said the young man, "we can not insure God, have a nice day." "That might be a bit disappointing," I said, "at least it didn't start off well." "Ah," the boy exclaimed who was clearly done with me, because he was already tapping his keyboard, "look at it this way, you could have been dead or your house badly damaged."

"You couldn't win here," I thought, turning around. "The boy looked up for a moment," if you need a chainsaw you can rent them at the end of the street, "and he turned back to the screen. I decided to go to the end of the street because I didn't have a chainsaw and I could always see what was for rent. I saw the store that hadn't previously registered with me because I hadn't needed any tools. Brightman's tool hire was on the door in big shining letters, I knew what time of day it was in this village.

The chain saw growled all day long and then the tree was cut to pieces and the side branches were lying on a pile outside my fence waiting for the municipal garbage disposal service to remove that kind of garden waste. When I walked to my garden gate for the umpteenth time with my arms full of smaller branches, I thought I had seen something from the corner of my eye as I passed the garbage cans. "Would I turn around," I thought, "and see if I was imagining things?" I heard a scraping sound and turned around in no time. For a moment I thought I saw a blue light above the garbage bin that was struck a short while later by a medium-sized branch that had come loose from between the shingles.

"Had I seen the bright blue light or not," I didn't know for sure, and then your memory starts to fill in what you may or may not have seen. At the same time as the branch that had been dumped on the garbage can, I had seen a blue glow or had it been a strange ray of sunshine that was troubling me. Had there been a vague outline, a shape vaguely visible as if it were about to break through. "I'm getting obsessed," I realized, "why did I hide what I might or might not have seen?"

Why didn't I just allow my inner voice to simply say, "I probably saw that unholy bowl?" I knew why I didn't allow that, somewhere in my head there was a warning, "if you name the bowl, then it becomes part of your reality with everything that goes with it and all the consequences that follow."

Did I allow myself to be influenced by my dreams and that bowl, which only exhaled negativity? I had followed an exact training in the past, I would not be guided by something that I conjured up myself, but ... but I did call the unpleasantness up myself or was the bowl only the medium, the tool of something even more devilish, an anchorage of the bad. Had the bad become connected to the bowl? "*Fear feeds fear,*" I knew from my past, and you should not allow that, but ... but what if the fear was real, did that rule still apply?

So deep in thought I arrived at the fence. "How are you," a voice sounded and I looked up. It was the racist neighbor. "Good, thank you and how are you," I replied.

"But it seems to me that my day has been more pleasant than yours." "Boy," I said, "tell me about it." "I have been working all day to clean up that tree." "Yes," I heard it, "he said," those trees have grown out of strength and a little wind is all it takes for them to fall over. "

"It was a big boy indeed," I laughed, my campfire can burn at least for a year. "You were lucky," grumbled my neighbor who had threatened Indians with guns only a few days beforehand. "I've seen people been carried away from your garden. You were lucky that the tree went during the night and not while you were in your garden, it was not for nothing that your house had been on sale for a few years." "Oh, that's new to me," I began, "the broker told me ..." but he interrupted, "brokers are like politicians or second-hand car sellers, they just want you to believe what they say." I nodded, I could picture that.

"Three owners have died in your house or nearby it," he laughed scornfully, "and I don't mean from old age. "Explain," I said more emphatically than I intended.

"The first one fell into the coal chute drunk as a skunk and when he tried to get out, the hatch that had been open fell shut. That chute was of course no longer used but the hatch had been open, why I do not know, but it must have been like that. He was a lonely man who wasn't missed and yes the gardens are big and deep. " I listened attentively and without me wanting to, I leaned over to the speaker not to miss a word.

"We had heard a dull pounding for days," my neighbor continued, "that must have been the poor bugger that was below the baseline in the chute and tried to attract attention. Look, that chute is about 4 meters deep, so you never get out of that funnel. After a while the banging ceased and only when the meter reader came to read the meter he smelled the stench of the decomposing corpse. "

  "It must have been terrible for that poor fellow," he concluded. "Phew," I said, "what a nasty story." "Yup," my neighbor said, "sure thing." "You get that from alcohol," my neighbor continued, "for a couple of months no meaningful word had come from that man, he uttered all sorts of nonsense about evil forces and drank more every day."

A long stretched shiver had slid down my spine. "Horrible," I said for something to say and for no other reason.

"Yeah," the neighbor continued, "the next owner was also a weird guy. He thought he heard murmuring voices, yes yes, you have all sorts of people in this village. " "Murmuring," I asked in shock, "where did he hear it." "Oh, everywhere behind the house," the neighbor grinned, showing little compassion for neighbors who had died. "A few meters from your house was a storage shed, where the concrete slab is now," and he pointed to what I had seen as an ordinary terrace.

"He had paint in it and a small workshop and fuel, some jerry cans with gas or something." "Yes," I said, "pounding again and such." "No, he had a strange obsession," laughed the man who started to scare me, "he thought there was a wandering light in his shed. "Sometimes with marshland you sometimes have false lights," my neighbor explained, "you know that, don't you?" I didn't know, but I nodded and decided to have a go at Google when I was back in.

"I told you," the neighbor went on, "you have all sorts of folk around here, so he wanted to catch it or something and he became stranger everyday and one afternoon when it was getting a little like dusk he walked into the shed smoking, he will have thought that the stray light was lit again and then it happened. " What exactly happened, "I wanted to know.

'I was mowing my lawn and I just happened to be doing a lane towards my fence and then I saw him walking into the shed smoking. I remember it exactly, I still see it as if it were yesterday that it happened. " "What happened," I said emphatically. "A flash of fire and an explosion that blew the side window out of the shed," said the neighbor who had watched, 'that is what you get when you walk into a fuel storage smoking.'

I immediately ran into the garden, but it seemed as if the door was jammed or locked from the inside. The paint cans were now exploding and I heard a whimpering scream coming out of the shed. Then I saw my neighbor burning like a torch trying to get out of the window and then he collapsed and I could do nothing. My neighbor looked into the distant past and was silent for a moment, "he was completely charred, you know."

"The last one, the one who bought the house before you bought it, heard voices in the garden and in the trees and out of anthills." "Good grace," I was able to say, "what a going on and, was that man burned too?" "He was crazy, my neighbor continued undisturbed," he claimed ants murmured. " "Eaten by ants," I tried to let my fear go away by making a stupid joke.

"No, a tree branch hit him on his head when he once again lay on his stomach and listened to ants." "Right," I said, "they've all had bad luck." "Yes," my neighbor said, "isn't that something hey?" "Boy," I said, "absolutely, what color are those false lights anyway?" "Blue of course," my neighbor laughed, "at least here in Saskatchewan, depends on the type of gas." "Thank you," I said, "my wife is waiting for me, I should go." "You do well to do so," my neighbor said, and as I approached the bins I made sure I did not step on the slab.

I decided to keep my neighbor's story to myself, why should I bother my partner with horror stories. "You seem a little absent," my wife said after I had been staring ahead of me for a while at the dinner table and was pondering over the misfortunes of my predecessors. "Yes, sure," I laughed, "that is what the cursed bowl does to you" " "At least it's over," she sighed, "I had another oppressive dream last night.

What do you say to the love of your life? You say, "Gosh, in what way oppressive?" "It was at the lake again," she began, "and there was a pounding or a drumming in the distance." I sat up straight away. "Voices," I asked? "Yes," she said in surprise, "more like a murmur, so you couldn't really understand what was being said." A shiver ran down my back. "Was there a strange light," I wanted to know. "I looked over the water and the sun came up," my wife continued, 'but it was different than usual. "How different," I asked.

"The sun was light blue," my sweetie told me, "and a moment later the bright blueness of that rising sun lighted up all the hills in hellish blue and in the meantime the pounding grew louder and the water called out to me and I knew for certain, as an undeniable truth, that if I were to go in, I would not ever come out again. " "If you feel so strong about something, it's a warning," I said to fill in the silence that had fallen. "I didn't want to go back to the beach," my dear said, "but I had to." "What makes you think so," I wanted to know. "Because the drum drew me forward," she said slowly, "and there was something behind me that was breathing heavily and everything turned dazzling blue, so bright blue that you had to shield your eyes with your hand."

"Forget it," I said emphatically, "dreams are but deceptions." Do you want some more coffee? ' "And what if dreams aren't deceptional," my wife continued, "and if you are really lured by the impure." "Is that how you experienced it," I asked, "as something impure." "Something demonically bad," my wife said, and I wish she hadn't used that word, but I knew fully well what she meant. "Let it go," I said, "I'll make you some more coffee, the bowl is gone and that's the end of it."

"You see," my wife continued, "you as well seem to believe that those strange dream images are brought about because of that bowl." "Let it go," I advised her again, but I knew she had expressed what I feared. "At the coffee machine the gravel voice sounded," *now we know it, don't we, the bowl is in you, you are the bowl.* I dropped the scoop in dismay and then wiped the worktop clean with the dish cloth. "Bugger off," I said to no one in particular. "What did you say," my wife asked sharply. "Nothing," I said, and I realized that I was the only one who had heard the gravel voice. With the second scoop of coffee my hand was slowly but surely turned over and that also ended up on the counter. "What are you doing," my wife asked surprised, "let me do it." A bit shaken I walked back to the table and then just before I sat down I thought something behind me was breathing heavily.

There was something wrong and, just like in the old days, if you were solving a difficult sum and took a little distance from the problem, you knew the answer was around the corner. Then the curtains of thought opened, and I knew what was wrong, my wife had embroidered on the dream she had had before, and the bowl had not been in the house anymore. Her subconsciousness had warned her for something demonic or was she lured by something that we do not want to recognize or discuss in modern day society.

"Oh my God," it dawned on me, I had received the bowl, had I really become the bearer of the bowl, whether it was present or not. Had I really heard the gravel voice or had it been my inner voice that had made an analysis of possibilities and considerations that we as modern humans do not allow in our thinking. Had I become the personification of what was wrong with that bowl? But why had I, except for the lake, incorporated the same elements and in my dream?

"The lake, water, *symbol of life*," it dawned on me and so the Historical Literature blocks that I had followed would have been good for something after all. But what about the cave, surely that wouldn't be a reference to Hades, the realm of mythology? "You look a little pale and you are very absent again," said the love of my life. "Why don't you go around the block and get a breath of fresh air, it will do you good."

My cup was ringing on my saucer, a heavy truck, had driven past and the streets had not been laid out for those in 1901. The large, freshly cut tree trunks protruded from the trunk and a red cloth fluttered at the end. "They are driving way too fast," my wife thought, "how should something like that ever make an emergency stop." I took my last sip of coffee and put my cup back on the saucer and got up to put it on the counter. My wrist started to lead a life of its own again and with great difficulty I was able to put it down safely.

"Thanks for the coffee," I said, "I will indeed take a walk down the street, I'll have a look at the Thriftstore of the Salvation Army, sometimes you come across nice second-hand items and you always help some charity anyway.' "I'll see you later then," said my sweetie, and she poured herself some more coffee.

The wind was blowing and my ears and nose were getting cold. "Does not surprise me," I thought, "they really do stick out." I pulled my neck in like a turtle and walked to the end of the street. At the parking lot of the Ford dealer I looked briefly at prices that were on F 150s. They did look tough, 1/2 ton of trucks with a double cabin and a large cargo bed. You saw half the village driving in them. "Goodness," I thought, "they started new at $ 80,000. You could buy a house for that sort of money, with a little luck." Even before I came to the corner, I knew something was wrong. A siren sounded and I saw all kinds of flashing lights.

When I came around the corner I froze. The lumber truck stood across the road and the thing that made me cringe the most was the right front wheel that was blocked by a half body, the rest was smeared over the asphalt like a bloody wipe. I could no longer move and something breathed in my neck and my inner voice, was it my voice, said, *"You see **you** are now the bringer of the blessings."* No I did not have a gravel voice, it had not been my voice. "I'm going crazy," I thought. "There is nothing to see here, please walk on," the officer said, very pale around his nose.

Then I saw the terrible thing a motorcycle lay underneath the truck at he back and floating, pierced by a thin tree trunk, a motorcyclist hung, he had been launched and the tree runk had speared him. "Oh man," I said, "what a misery" " F..ing Indian people," said an old man, "they just don't pay attention and just cross over whenever they feel like it." Then I saw the empty plastic bottles scattered everywhere on the street and I just had the idea where the Indian had taken them from. I stumbled into the Thriftstore and Les, the manager, "said," that would be two less. "What do you mean by two," I wanted to know? The speared one is the brother of the smeared out Indian, "that God may have their souls," he said piously.

I felt dizzy and heard a distant rumble as if drums were being struck. It is my heart that is pounding in my ears, I told myself and then Les pushed me into a chair. "Alright big boy don't faint," he said, "take a deep breath and look at your shoes," and I did. The blue glow of the light beam on the police car cast a pulsating spooky light in the store. "The fire department is already coming," Les said, "they'll hose the street down. The sounds became a murmur and my heart was beating in my ears and I looked at my shoes with my head in my hands.

When I walked out of the Thriftstore I had two books under my arm and there was only a wet street staring at me. Less had been very nice, "I'll make you some tea," he had said, "and you have to feel a little less concerned with the misery we see every day, whatever happens, there is always a reason." That was just the point, I was convinced that what was taking place had a reason. I sincerely doubted my sanity, why should I not have given my inner voice a gritty effect if I half and half expected that I would hear such a thing.

In the room behind the store I heard a tap running and I realized that the tea was being made fresh. I decided to make a list of everything that had come to pass. Two ladies had come by and they had left a gift. The one lady had said that she always acted on instructions from the Spirit, and I had assumed that she meant the Holy Spirit and that she was quite confused. She reported that voices gave her instructions, for example to put on a certain item of clothing. There was something else, oh yes, "the gift had more to do with the location," she had said, "than with the recipient." If you looked at that in retrospect, not much had happened, and if it were so, why would I have had such an *unheimlich* feeling about the bowl.

I reasoned that away, feelings are feelings and those are moments that we evoke ourselves. Sitting in an easy chair in the store of the Salvation Army, waiting for a cup of tea, it all didn't seem that mystifying anymore. Then I had gone to Saskatoon to visit my nephew and after we had gone home, three neighbors sank through the ice while ice fishing and drowned. Is that really so bizarre? Every year people sink through the ice and drown, unfortunately that will always be the case. I had a nightmare and my wife had had one as well, those are things that occur, that is not so extraordinary, everyone sometimes has a nightmare and I reasoned a lot away and I felt a bit more cheerful.

From hearsay, from a neighbor I had heard a strange story about what had happened to the previous three owners of my house. How had that discussion

begun? I knew it again, a tree had landed in my garden after it had fallen over. Every day trees are blown over with a bit of wind, probably a tree will blow over somewhere at any given time of the day. Maybe some of us are collectors, I thought and we charge ourselves, be it with positive things or with negative things.

I felt a lot calmer and looked around me. Household items donated by heirs of deceased loved ones were piled up. Next to me stood a huge pile of bibles, in all shapes and sizes, from paperback edition to thick well-read copies. Here and there were some clothes racks and shelves full of cups, saucers, and glasses and shelves full of books. I caught myself looking to see if there was a blessing bowl somewhere. To be honest, I was looking for my bowl. Les came back with a tray with two cups of tea and a bowl with sugar and a milk jug. "I like my tea black," I reported, and he looked at me with a punitive look.

"That's not very healthy, you know," he said, filling my cup up. "I know," I explained, "but I just like tea without milk and sugar." "At least you've got some color back," he smiled, "you looked like you'd seen a ghost." I nodded, "I feel better, a little calmer," and I took a careful sip of tea.

"Less," I said, "do you believe in unholy things, such as demons, for example." "This is the store of the Salvation Army," he began, "and I am a Salvation Soldier, a Christian," naturally I believe in demons. " "Because ...," I asked? Because our Lord Jesus often speaks about demons in the Bible, "he said as if he was explaining something to a stupid child."

"Jesus said:" When an unclean spirit leaves someone, he travels through arid places in search of a resting place. But if he does not find it, he says, "I will return to my house that I have left behind." He will then arrive with 7 new demons that are worse than himself, and they will all stay there permanently. And so, after all, the person with whom the demon moves in is much worse off than before. That is how it will be ".

That comes from the Bible, Les explained, "Matthew 12: 43-45." "I'm not that biblical," I replied, "but I understand that as a Christian, you follow Jesus Christ and therefore his statements." "You can count on that.. Yes Sir," Les said. "Next to you is a pile of bibles, we always give them away for free, take one if you want to." "No," I said, "thank you, if I ever need one, I'll come by." "I can't force you," Les said kindly, "do whatever you think is wise."

"Speaking of books," I said, "I see that you have a lot of 2nd hand books for sale, have you got something, you know, about dream interpretation or demons." "We don't do demons," the Thriftstore boss said, "but there is a book about dreams," and he got up and came back with two books. "This is your dream book," he said, holding up a book, "and this is a book about cursed objects, a bit demonic, I think." What do they cost, "I asked. "Just give me a dollar and I'll be rid of them." I popped up a dollar coin and gave it to the biblical versed owner.

"You don't want a free Bible," he sighed, "but false books suit you!" "I'm happy about it, and that's what it's about," I laughed. "Another question," I continued, "have you been offered a blessing bowl." "The Lord blesses his creation," Les said resolutely, "no one needs a bowl or plate or anything else." "Thank you," I said, "you helped me a lot with the tea and the Matthew story and all that.

"It was just before you came in that a bowl was sold," Les told, "a gloomy looking bowl." "To whom did you sell it," I asked fiercely. "Ah, to an Indian from the reservation," Les said, "the bowl appealed to him," he said. "Right," I said, "thanks again and I have to go. "Have a nice day," said the soldier of God, "and you," I replied.

The street was sprayed wet and shone at me, *there we are again*," the gravel voice spoke next to me and I almost dropped the books in dismay. My ratio told me that as long as I had sat next to a pile of bibles in a shop of the Salvation Army, I could feel calm and reason everything away, but there is always more than one truth and I knew that when I was back in the cold outside world.

My way led me back along the parcel of trucks and, lost deeply in thought, I didn't as much as glance. I stepped away per step from the speared Indian and before I knew it I was standing at my front door. My home wifi made my cell phone vibrate and I saw the message that came up. It was my sweetheart who told me that she was drinking coffee with friends at the Round up. The Round up was a place where the ranchers wives went for coffee and where cowboys and cowpokes gathered.

It opened early in the morning and by European standards, that was really early. Her doors opened six o'clock in the morning and the men had their bite to eat, a typical Western breakfast consisting of eggs, bacon, tomatoes, sausages and hash browns, which were small potato pieces. It was a hearty breakfast, but if you sit on a horse for hours at a time to round cattle up or to keep them down while branding, you may want something solid in your stomach. The men always sat together at a long table and a girl walked by with endless refills of coffee that were free.

She'd walk by with the pot in her hands and looked questioningly at you and if you then pushed your mug slightly towards her, it was immediately refilled. Later in the day people would have homemade apple pie there, but the early morning was for the men who needed a good bite to round 'em up.

The women came early as well and sat at another long table and so it had become a social meeting place.

The conversations were without exception about the harvests, the livestock or the politicians who had no regard for the farmers. That was a real problem, 48% of the Canadians lived in the French-speaking part and Saskatchewan had only 1 million inhabitants. About as much as its neighboring farmers province, Manitoba. Saskatchewan was one of the scarce sites where Uranium was found on the globe, which was used for nuclear power plants or nuclear weapons. On the other side to the West, Alberta bordered our province with its 4 million inhabitants. It was rich in oil, producing more of the black tea than all of Texas. The most Western province was British Columbia, it had 5 million inhabitants. She had the monopoly in the fisheries. With a total of 37 million inhabitants, Canada was sparsely populated. It was the second largest country in the world surpassed only by Russia and 48% of its population lived in the East, in the French part.

The complaints at the coffee table were with a good cause. If the East had voted, then the whole West could stay at home, because their votes were not going to change anything, and the farmers were right about that, the old farmers knew how it worked. I started to read up on Canadian politics on the internet because I didn't want to look stupid at the coffee table among all those rough hard-working men. I read that an equalization tax formula was used to levy taxes. It had been intended in the distant past, 150 years ago, to roughly equalize the Canadian infrastructure.

Richer states therefor paid more taxes to provide poorer states with a good health care system or road network. Like all laws, they are, in essence, well-intentioned, but over time, they are then misused by cunning politicians, and such was the case in Canada as well. Because of its oil wealth, Alberta contributed 13% to the national budget with only 10% of the working population. The Uranium profits from Saskatchewan followed the same path. Ditto with the income from the fisheries or the grain harvests.

Manitoba, Saskatchewan, Alberta and British Columbia who paid the bulk of the national budget received nothing in return. No improvements, no subsidies, they had just become milking cows. Where was the budget being spent? It can be guessed, in the East and a good 81% of it. The other 19% went to Indian territories (they can also vote, so a billion here or there does attract people). It did not come as a surprise that the prime minister was French, "Justin Trudeau," and that he is seen as the great benefactor in the area where 48% of the population lives.

Regardless of the linguistic struggle and the difference in culture between the West and the East, it is very difficult to pay taxes, get nothing in return, and have that money invested in the area that already has the most industry. After my internet crash course in Canadian politics, I understood the resentment that prevailed at the coffee table with the farmers who worked hard every day without the support of the Central Government. "*Trudeau is a sissy,*" an old farmer had explained to me, " *a real pussy,*" he has never sat on a horse." Another man with a gigantic cowboy hat and a deeply grooved face nodded, "he doesn't know that we exist, but he exists by the grace of us." "*He's a wanker,*" a third farmer had expressed his opinion, "he's dances about with Indians in a dress. Just for the votes, *he is a bloody poofter*. " I had thought that world-wide politicians did not differ that much.

That's where my sweety was now, in the Round up, probably having a mug of coffee, at the ladies' table, while the cowboys at the other table complained themselves silly. I put the key in the lock and opened the front door, half and half expecting to hear a bongo drumming, but that was not the case. I did hear a murmur of voices from the bedroom and for a moment my heart skipped a few beats. I exhorted myself and before I got really scared I was heading for the bedroom, I pushed the door open and there was nothing. With a sigh of relief I saw that the radio alarm clock was on, and voices came pouring out softly. I was there with two steps and turned it off. "I must not let myself go funny," I thought, "not necessary, I am doing it already to myself,

I just smiled for a second. Most events in this life have an ordinary rational explanation. "Just reason it away," my inner voice said reprovingly. "That is so much more pleasant than accepting that there are simply inexplicable things in this world that do not fit in with the rational world that we love so much." That was my own inner voice, I recognized it immediately. God Almighty I had already reached the point where I was having a discussion with my inner voice which was myself!

But was that not always the case, our thoughts are always formed in language. "No, that was wrong," I knew for certain. In linguistic blocks that I had followed in the distant past, this had frequently been discussed. We process abstract matters and come out and formulate them in language if we want to transfer our thoughts to a listener, when I think of a hospital for instance, I see a 'gestalt', an image of white coats, long corridors with running people, a reception , a concoction of things that we catch under the heading: hospital. "Pretty, clever," I thought, "we print a few letters over an image that is very complex, we do think in terms of images."

So we think in images and sometimes in language because we have been trained that way. I went to the coffee machine and put in the capsule that would deliver me a café solo far away in Canada. My cell phone in my pocket vibrated for a moment. "*You thought a button would solve everything,*" the gravel voice asked, and I almost dropped the water jug. I banished the voiceout with all my power and looked at the screen of my cell phone. Nothing but nothing had been received.

"*Hold it to your ear,*" gravel voice now emphatically advised me and I followed his order. "*Now you can hear me more clearly.*" it sounded scratchy. "*Pay attention,*" he advised me, and I was petrified by not calling anyone and yet hearing people talking. "There was a single tap first, and then a slow drumming and a murmur of voices that were indistinguishable, and then a connection lost tone. With horror, I slipped the cell phone into my pocket and pressed the red 'on' button and the obedient coffee machine started sputtering. At least no voices were being cast here. "Don't go there," I thought, "don't even allow such a thought, not even as a joke."

The biblical creation story that I had heard in a very distant past, long ago far away from Canada and café solos and demonic gravel voices at Sunday school, came to the surface. "And God said, Let there be light! and there became light. " That came from the book of Genesis I remembered. There the word became reality.

I didn't want any murmur voices to come out of my coffee machine. So I shouldn't even think about it, God knows what we can all shape, project or evoke. One just has to let the genie out of the bottle, so to speak, and hope that one will remain the boss of their own actions. I was amazed to see how my hand held the cup over the counter and while I resisted, my wrist led a life of its own and the cup poured neatly out over the drain. "*Just for the sake of clarity,*" it sounded from my expresso machine, accompanied by a soft rumble that died away. I sat down at my table and only after a few seconds did I notice that I was looking out through the back window without recording anything and that I rocked back and forth rhythmically, autistically.

"Nothing wrong," I reminded myself, "I think in voices and that is not extraordinary, the ratio was once again the force majeure before I would again slip into the shadow world. I took out my cell phone and went to Google. "hearing voices," I typed. The number of sites that were about hearing voices surprised me. It was apparently common, it could not always be explained. Sometimes it was accompanied by a medical condition.

I learned that many people heard voices and that you could give it a place. You had to become the boss over the voice so that you could silence it. I had once bought a Volkswagen and that day I saw a lot of Volkswagens driving around. Your focus is therefore determined by your own experiences. I had never been much interested in hearing voices, but it was not unknown to me that such an issue existed, there were entire scientific sites that were concerned with hearing voices.

Prophets were guided by a voice. Moses, the man who led the people of Israel out of exile, heard a voice from a bramble bush and that was thousands of years ago, so people had been hearing at least voices for thousands of years. Yes, so who is crazy and who is normal, or are there only gradations of normality with outliers on the spectrum from crazy to reasonably normal, who sets the standard?

I read and read and tried to put it into words for myself. " Our memory is fantastic. Often a part of a word, a sound or an object is enough for us to know what it is. We have developed expectation patterns. We hear the difference between an engine of a truck or a moped. When we see a petal, we know that it is part of a whole flower and we can visualize the entire image. We can even form an image with a sound or an odor. So you don't have to see something to be able to imagine it.

Your memory fills the image up with your imagination. Sometimes you are convinced that you have seen or heard something, but in reality your imagination has supplemented your perception with the complete image from your memory. Your expectation plays a major role in this: you do not expect to see a moped when you hear a large truck. For people who hear voices, supplementing perception plays a major role. In fact, their memory supplements the perception faster. This ensures that they are often super alert and respond quickly to sounds or events. They can misinterpret an incentive and therefore see or hear something different than there is in reality. This is called auditory hallucination. "

I now started to doubt where I stood in this story, I had always thought that I had been a fairly normal person, but probably everyone thinks that. *"Learning to deal with the voices in your head,"* I read, "also means that you learn to listen to the voices in a different way. It can be very frightening when you hear voices that instruct you to do something or that speak to you roughly. In therapy, many people discover that the voices in their heads are trying to tell them something. By talking to a counselor about the voices, they can find out what the meaning is. A special interview method has even been developed for this. '

I'm not going to go that way, I decided, before you know it you're under the pills or in an asylum. "Hearing voices is different for everyone. Some people hear a voice once in their life for a shorter period, others hear several different voices throughout the day. Voices that talk to each other, voices that are helpful or aggressive. Someone who hears voices does not necessarily have to be psychotic and someone who is psychotic does not have to hear voices. Psychosensitive people hear relatively more voices than people who are not psychosensitive. A worldwide network of voice hearers and aid workers has since been established; the hearing voices movement. "

"Nice to know," I thought, "I won't do anything with that." I was, however, somewhat reassured that very many people heard voices.

The soft drumming dawned on me and I knew where it came from, the bedroom. Just when I wanted to go there, it stopped at the same time as the sound of a key being stuck in the front door. "Hi," my love said, "have you been here a long?" "No, not really," I replied "was it fun at the Roundup?"

"Not really," she replied, "an accident had happened and everyone was talking about it and, worst of all, Les from the Thrift Shop had a stroke, he was found by a customer in the kitchen." "How sad," I said, wondering why my wife and I were still alive, and then I knew why, the dish was given to our location, we were the designated bearers of the dish. That holy and terribly unholy thing, that only meant death and destruction for those who were not called to the bowl, could not be touched without being punished.

"Not bad, for a newby," said the gravel voice. I ignored the voice. "Gee," I said, "poor Les, he helped me pick two books and then he still looked healthy, but you never know what is around the corner." "What happened to the woman in black who brought me the bowl," I asked half aloudand lost in thought. "Did you say something," my wife asked, taking off her coat. "Oh, I muttered something in myself," I said, "I have had that lately." My dear boy, "she said, stroking my hair for a moment," you had a senior moment. *" she was absorbed into the noble nothingness,* "the gravel voice sounded. "Did you hear something," I asked my wife. "No," she said, "why." "Never mind," I replied, "Just my imagination," but I knew what time of day it was.

"Maybe I want to approach it all too intellectually," I thought, "maybe life is a chaos and you just have to accept that, without asking too many questions, You mustn't want to understand everything. Okay there had been a few deaths, a soldier from the Salvation Army had suffered a stroke, three previous owners had not survived the purchase of our house. In itself, all that was still acceptable in a normal framework, of reality as we accept it. "

"Hello have you gone mad," my inner voice called out to me, almost furiously! 'You know, you really know how it really is. You were approached, you were chosen by something or whatever, your wrist was taken possession of. Soon it may be your whole body, it invades your dreams and inflicts harm on people around you, hello are we awake again! I was awake but pushed my alter ego away. I didn't want to know or ponder. "You are having one of your days again," my dear said, "you are very quiet lately." "I think a lot of late," I answered truthfully. "About life in general and whether our society is just a thin shell of civilization with hidden beneath it, in layers, primal forces of which we have forgotten the existence of."

"Those are deep thoughts for such a beautiful clear day as today," my dear laughed. "Maybe you can get the bins in before dark. It gets dark so quickly here. " She was right about that, the evening fell fast and the thought made me shiver just like that, how would I sleep, if at all, wouldn't I be lured into dark caves again?

"Of course I will get them in," I said. 'You are right you know kids might mess them about if we leave them out,' but in reality, my other reality, I thought of the two Indians who had dug through our bin and most likely had found the bowl and had touched it, and had carried it between the empty plastic bottles and were now flat out in the morgue with a litlle name card from their toe. As far as the smeared out Indian would still have had a toe.

On the other side of the alley, past the garbage cans, I saw my neighbor dragging a ladder to the backside of his house. I watched him through the window facing the backyard for a moment, he carefully lowered the ladder and slowly climbed up it. When he was at the top he put his left hand in the gutter and pulled out a handful of leaves. I saw that his left hand was light yellow.

"He put on a washing up glove," I realized. He descended again and shifted the ladder a meter and climbed up again to repeat the ritual. He immediately descended again and tilted the ladder a little more. Then he went up carefully again. "He does well," I thought, "he takes no risks." I put on my coat and walked to the back garden and froze in the middle of a step, because I thought I'd had seen a fleeing dark shape near the large pine tree. Sometimes you have that, you think that you have seen something from the corners of your eyes. I noticed that it had been running from the coal chute, which now had a padlock on the hatch, to the tree. I shook it off and continued my walk towards the back gate.

I heard heavy breathing behind me and then one drum beat. I almost let out a scream of fright. I changed my direction as if I was walking to my shed but the breathing went with me. It was not my own breath because if I held my breath, the slow, heavy breathing still continued very close behind me. Suddenly I turned around in a flash and I saw a black shadow rush away and I didn't know why, but I was almost sure it was a female form. Not the dark-looking woman who had donated the dish, she had, by the way, been absorbed into the noble nothingness, or the oblivion or just give it a name, according to my house demon. All in all I had started to cite the gravelvoice as confirmation of things I didn't know how they had taken place.

The pool of oblivion, that was something from my study many years ago, from Historical literature, I decided to google it later, it had been so, so very long ago that I had followed those lectures, something from Greek myths, I thought. "Narcissus," I suddenly knew with certainty.

The shadow shrank and turned into a black ball that raced past me and then took a bump over the fence and I knew what was going to happen and I saw the black ball grow again and I held my hand in front of my mouth, I appeared to be nailed down. It increased in speed and toppled the ladder. Then two drum beats and an evil laughter and the black ball dissolved. "Into noble oblivion," I thought.

I saw my neighbor, who had been so careful, half turn over in his fall as he smashed down on his wheelbarrow with a cracking sound, and what stuck to me was the unnatural position of his leg that, like that of a play doll, was folded under him and his neck that pointed to his house in an impossible angle. I ran back home and yelled at my wife, "Call an ambulance, the neighbor fell off the ladder," and I ran back to my negative neighbor. But I already saw it, a negative story would never pass his lips again.

I stood by the remains of my neighbor, just so that no animal or whatever else could disturb him. It was not long before an ambulance entered the alley and stopped when I beckoned him beside me. "There he is," I said, pointing to the shape that lay next to the wheelbarrow. A paramedic rushed around the ambulance and ran to what had been my neighbor. He looked almost compassionately at the man, "he is gone," he said, "just to make sure," he listened to the chest, felt the wrist. "No breathing and no heartbeat," he said dryly. "We can't take him with us," he continued, "regulations, hey." "I'll warn the police and the hearse, will you stay with him for a little longer?"

And without waiting for my answer he walked to the car and got in and started calling and so they drove away leaving me with what had been the negative neighbor. I picked up the trash cans and in turn rolled them through my gate to their place behind the house. In the meantime, I was watching my dead neighbor. The car with the red and blue lights stopped next to me. RCMP was written on the side in large letters. "You've come, let's say, for my neighbor," I asked, and the man nodded from behind his wheel.

"That's where he is," I pointed out, "he fell down a ladder." The driver stopped beside me and the second man walked over to the corpse. "You are," he asked me, and when I had answered him, he asked, "you saw it all," which I answered in the affirmative. "He lost his balance, I just walked up to the alley to get the bins." "Well," the man said, "things like that happen, you can go, we know where to find you if we have any more questions." He resolutely turned around and went to his colleague.

"How is it," my wife asked as I stepped inside. "Not too good," I said, "he's stone dead, I think he has broken his neck." She looked at me in dismay. "Such a nice man," she said, "he always gave me a wave when I hung up the washing." "Yup," I said, "he liked to have his little chat," and I thought how strange is it, when you are dead, people forget that you were always a racial obsessed fellow with hateful remarks and everyone only remembered nice stuff about you. "The hearse is coming soon," I continued, "the ambulance may not let's say, transport dead patients."

That evening we sat up for a while and followed with half an eye a series about a horse ranch. After the series had come to a successful conclusion, the horse thief was caught and everyone was happy again, we went to bed. I walked past the front door and checked if it was locked and when that turned out to be the case I went to brush my teeth. It had been a turbulent day. Smeared out and speared Indians, a salvation army soldier who had suffered a stroke, a story about the miserable end of the previous three owners of our building and last but not least, the narrator of that story who was fatally bowled over by a black figure, but then really as if we had been in a bowling alley. So we lay quietly next to each other and then I turned off the reading light. "Night sweety," I said, turning around.

'I was at my sister's and we were enjoying a cup of tea. We were in the old kitchen and I felt relaxed. "Hey," said my sister, " did you hear that," and I stiffened because a rumble had started under our feet. "What do you mean," I asked as innocently as possible? "Then listen," she said, "it seems to come from under the floor." Then a slow roar began, and I suspected that the small basement below her house would probably be bathed in bright blue light by now. "Let's take a look," my sister said, putting her cup on the table and walking to the end of the kitchen where there was a hatch in the floor with a ring on it. "Don't open the hatch," I called to my sister as I quickly got up to pull her away from the hatch, "there's something *unholy* in your basement ... the crackling died away slowly."

"It's a dream," I thought, "don't give in," I'm in control, I'm in bed. *'We'll see, about that',* a gravel voice sounded and I went down my basement stairs in my own house and I heard the rhythmic drumming and it lured me to the far side of the cellar where my workshop was. The door was half open and a bright blue light shone out and I heard the voice, the voice of my recently deceased neighbor, who said, "He's almost here, just wait a little longer."

I certainly did not want to go to the bright blue light that fell out of the open door, and certainly not when I recognized my neighbor's voice. But just as my wrist had poured out my coffee, my legs refused to obey me. I wanted to turn around but again I did not dare to stand with my back to the light and I struggled with forces that lured me and my ego and the rationality that forbade me to continue. The rhythm of the drum slowed down and now and again and then grew stronger and then weaker as if carried on the wind. I knew what would follow, the murmuring, it was always like that. The drumming won over me and I gradually shuffled towards the light. The drumming stopped for a moment and I heard my sister's voice above me, she asked someone something.

"Hey," said my sister, "can you hear that?" The voice that answered was my voice. "What do you mean," I asked. Good God I was in two places at the same time, that couldn't be true. But I saw my workshop door come closer and I knew for sure that I was in my basement. "No," thought my rational being, "no and again no, it has nothing to do with where I am, it is like abstracting and pasting words over images, it is about the concept of a cellar, this is done because of me in cellars . "

I looked up and saw neither the hatch under my sister's kitchen nor the stairs that would lead me upstairs. I was in the basement as a concept, and against my will I was taken somewhere by something demonic. It started to get warmer around me and I was pulled forward to that warmth and when I almost got to the door I got a silly thought. "I could do with some sunglasses," the basement began to deform and became granite.

With the greatest possible effort, I held back and even managed to walk a few steps back. The granite disappeared and I was clearly in an old cellar again. That only lasted a moment, I heard a deep breath coming after me and catching up and so I quickly stepped forward again. " Just with my luck "I thought ,"the dark one will come forward from the shadows again and then do someone in.' That was the last thing I wanted.

Now the granite became more rounded and the drumming had grown in strength. I walked into what was slowly becoming a cave and at the end on the right hand side I saw what had been a door, slanting open on old hinges and bright light was being cast in. My last sensible thought when I stepped through the door was, "A cave is a cellar and a cellar is a cave, both dark and gloomy," and then I stood in the light and it engulfed me and blinded me and I only heard a murmur that seemed to come from afar. I could not make anything out, my eyes had to get used to the warm bright light.

"There you are, you see it wasn't that far after all, now was it" my neighbor's voice said, "now you are at the intersection and **that** is what it is all about." I was being shaken hard, "wake up San," my sweety said, "you only moan and you only utter cries and nonsense. She turned on the night light and I came from far away from hellish bright beacons and cave vaults into my safe world.

"San, just look at yourself," she said, "you're soaking wet," you have to clean up first. Do you want some water? ' So many words at once, so much care, but the images, because we do think in images, were still etched in my soul, they did not evaporate to dissolve into meaningless fragments. I had been at the point of intersection whatever that might be. "By the way," said my sweety, "who is the black woman you keep shouting at." Someone very scary, "I replied, and I noticed that my pyamas were indeed sticking to me.

In the morning with a cup of tea, I let my mind wander again over the nightly experiences. It was no small matter if your neighbor, who had not been dead for a day, spoke to you in your cellar or cave or whatever the room was. The heat had almost been tropical and I remembered that I had thought about sunglasses. What exactly had my deceased neighbor said, something in the spirit of crossing lines, no, he had said an intersection. But what was that supposed to mean and why all that blinding light.

Bright blue as if someone was welding and you were watching it without eye protection. I took my faithful cell phone and went to Google. "Crossing, oh no," I corrected myself and typed in intersection.

I knew what an intersection was, but I wanted to have the definition and not rely on what I remembered from geometry. It seemed important to me to see what my neighbor really had said. I just had the idea that in the cave life words were weighed and really had meaning. Internet is a miracle box and a moment later I read what the geometric definition of an intersection was.

'An intersection of two curves is a point in geometry that lies on both curves. It is the point where the curves intersect. More than two curves can also have a common intersection. "

That was not new to me and I could picture that. Here too was another representation of an abstract thought that had been given a name, "intersection." Just a common point where two lines crossed. –

Two straight lines in a flat plane intersect exactly once or not at all. In the latter case, parallel lines are used. There are spaces where two lines can intersect more than once. "

This was, in my opinion, a representation of a two-dimensional world view. For example a square, only length and width and no depth.

A flat dimension that did not display depth. "Two randomly chosen lines in a three-dimensional space generally do not intersect." "A cube," I thought, "for example, it is three-dimensional. It has a depth, length and width.

Three-dimensional means that something has three dimensions. ... Spatial figures in mathematics exist in a three-dimensional space. '

"I'm going to the Roundup," my sweety said, "are you coming too?" I was torn away from reflections on intersections and three or two dimensional spaces and what could or could not occur there.

"I want to finish my reading," I answered her. "Maybe I'll come later." "She smiled sweetly at me," you should know that yourself, "she thought," but don't wait too long if you do want to come. " I blew her a kiss and turned my eyes back to the small screen. " Moments later I heard the heavy Chrysler move away and the rumbling sound faded into the distance. What had dead neighbor said, exactly said, before I was woken up? "

"Now you are at the intersection and **that**'s what it's all about." he had said that literally. It seemed like he was explaining why I was drawn to that particular place. But I had not seen an intersection, I could not see anything in seriousness because of the bright blinding light. The crux was something that he designated as an intersection, what then cut through which point?

He seemed to think it was very important. What came together there. Had it been intended literally or communicatively? For example, had he referred to different dimensions, or time segments intersecting there. Or or or. In my workplace, which transformed last night into a cave, there was apparently a point of intersection of something that was extremely important, because my neighbor had said ... "and that's what it's all about." A curve or a line or a dot are but representations of abstract possibilities that exist in a space. Was it a meeting point of two worlds, or of a force field, was that what he wanted to say? He had not simply used the intersection, what if he had only meant: the intersection of two world views, of two dimensions. Good God and that under my house.

It did explain why the two bringers of the bowl had said that it was not so much about the owner as about the location when they had given me the bowl. A short tap on a drum sounded from under my feet, for a moment I wondered if I had actually heard it, but that didn't last long because a voice spoke to me. "*Did you really think we would let you go?*" The gravel voice paused briefly and then continued, "*All you had to do was bring the bowl and you lost it.*"

I listened petrified and the fingers of my left hand began to drum nervously on the table without me wanting it. "*We even brought you to the location,*" screeched gravel voice, "and you turn up empty-handed. *We can do something about that. Are you attached to your hands? How about your right hand in the meat grinder? ' Take a look at your right hand!* " I couldn't think anymore and I saw how my right hand first picked up the tea mug and then squeezed it.

It shattered and two earthenware pieces went into my hand. "*Do you want to know what your hand will look like when the grinder is done, do you like minced meat.*" I could only shake no, because I already envisioned my left hand working the grinder. I got up and said aloud, I am going to the Roundup. I began to hum and did not allow any thought or voice to enter my head and cleared the shards. I wiped the table with a cloth and held my hand under the tap and tore a piece off the kitchen roll and wrapped it around my hand to stop the bleeding. I put my coat on and walked out of the door.

The round up was as always the round up. I was sitting at the table with the cowboys who complained about the government and none of them had been dealing with demons in a cave for the night. So I listened to yet another story about the government and how unfairly it treated our province.

The girl with the coffee pot came by several times for the refill and after a while I thought it was enough and I decided to go home. My wife was still sitting at her coffee table, I waved at her and walked to the counter to pay. I thought about going to the basement when I was at home, but I decided not to do that, there was too much that had upset me in the basement and I didn't feel safe there. I wanted to look up some things in the books I had received from Les and the internet should fill in any gaps.

Walking home I let my mind wander again about the last night. I had come to the point where I had come to regard the nightmares as real. It was a glimpse into another reality. I also considered throwing the meat grinder away, but realized that the gravel voice could probably harm me in many other ways. I just saw in a flash how he let me hold my hand over the gas stove while I screamed in pain. "Don't," I thought, "don't go there, you are filling your head with assumptions." Humming had helped, it had occupied my mind so that nothing else was allowed in. I hummed *Sympathy for the devil of the Stones*.

Not a happy choice I thought and I smiled for a moment, "oh well we could still laugh at all the fear." When I got home I walked directly to the table, to the two books that I got from the salvation army soldier. "Dream interpretation," lay on top, so fate had decided I thought. It was alphabetical to consult, so I went to the "C" of cave. " Dreaming that you are walking in a dark cave, "I read," is an exploration of your subconscious. It indicates self-discovery. "

"That's nice," I thought, "what do I discover or is it an attempt to think outside the box?" I went on to the 'V' of voices. "Hearing voices in your dream," the book told me, "means a message from the subconscious or spiritual realm." "Hmm," I thought, "was the gravel voice coming from my subconscious for God knows what reason," or did it come from the spiritual realm? " I determined from the spiritual realm, for I would never consider grinding my right hand with my left hand. What was the message then, or was it a feeling that warned me and revealed itself as a voice? The grinding had been a threat.

Why should I threaten myself? It had been the result of not bringing the bowl to the location. As a kind of punishment. I didn't want the dish. I had not thrown it away.

So a power from outside of myself threatened me. Manipulated my hands so that my wrist did not obey me and destroyed anyone who had not been called to the bowl. But how could I have known in my dream that I should have taken the bowl, moreover, that was not even possible, because an Indian had bought the bowl and taken it to the reservation.

The two Indians who had taken it out of my garbage had rushed towards their accident, one had ended in speared and the other was spread out on a road half. "Goodness," I thought, "what would be happening on the reservation now?" Would they all get the plague or be killed by a bunch of buffalos?

The bowl was clearly the catalyst of everything that had happened to me in recent days and apparently it had to be placed at the intersection, whatever that was, and that would solve everything, because my dead neighbor had said 'and **that** is what it is all about.' As if the bowl was a connecting key between worlds, the bowl was the intersection, or an intersection in time or between dimensions, I realized, or together with an intersection that gave bright light, a wholenes of some sort. Was the gravel voice a part of the bowl or was it a demon who was in the service of a higher power, to get me the owner of the location to put the "key," in the "lock,"?

My head was spinning but I knew I had come a long way, I had weighed and weighed and although I could not discuss it with anyone, I had unraveled part of the puzzle and a rational emerged. The bowl had to go to an intersection. That intersection had to do with a location. The scale probably had an appearance or a load that was needed to lock or unlock the intersection. Indeed a kind of lock with a key, I thought satisfied, whether open or closed, or accessible or not.

The position now was clearly the 'not position' and all kinds of dark forces thought it was necessary for that position to change and I was the owner of the location. The dream book was useful, I consulted my characteristics from those symbols that countless people had dreamed before me. So I went to the 'w' of water, because my love had dragged by a current in a lake and oh well you are curious and want to know if it means something at all.

Seeing water in your dream symbolizes your subconscious mind and your emotional state, "I read. Water is the living essence of the psyche and the flow of life energy. It is also a symbol of spirituality, knowledge, healing and refreshment.

"Well, we know a bit more now," I thought, "although here too it was about refreshing thoughts, awakening or being open to, and again the spirituality." This is no coincidence, "I knew," what is the chance that two people in a bed, dream about a theme that symbolically embraces the same. " We were being influenced, there was no other way about it.

"Then lets do the colors," I decided, looking at light in dreams and especially bright light and blue. 'Seeing light in your dream stands for lighting, clarity, guidance, clear understanding and insight. Light is shed on a once cloudy situation or problem. You have found the truth about a situation or an answer to a problem. Also consider the color of the light for extra meaning .... Dreaming of a bright light coming from an object often means divinity and / or a higher consciousness. Consider the meaning of the object and its role in your spirituality or spiritual journey. " I thought dream interpretation was no longer ridiculous.

Again the spirituality, the budding understanding. When I searched for the color blue, I came up with the colors of the virgin Mary, Blue and white, and oblivion, "I did not exactly have the idea that the Blessed Virgin was in my basement, but then I read on and I read read, "blue symbolizes stillness and infinity." Would you unconsciously sense things for which you needed a book to put it into words? I didn't know but suddenly I no longer considered the dream symbolism nonsense.

I had more or less expected an admonishing voice, gritty in nature, but it remained calm in my head. Maybe I had already banned my demon out while humming and I shouldn't have thought that. It was requesting the devil and that saying did not exist for nothing in our language. A short beat sounded and my inner voice had become rough and gritty and I knew what was wrong. My inner voice was repressed, from now on the rough voice would accompany my thoughts. "What had been said again," I thought with the gravel voice of my demon who had really become my demon now.

I was being watched and had not complied with transferring the bowl at the intersection point, whatever that meant. "Ha," I thought, "games are being played with me," my inner voice has become the gravel voice but, I don't know what the intent of the intersection debacle is, and if the demon had really sailed into me, my thoughts uttered by my inner voice would have known. " "*Why haven't you asked me, if you wanted to know*," the rough voice sounded. "I couldn't have imagined that," I realized, and I almost whispered, "what is the purpose of the intersection?" "*The homecoming, of course*," the voice growled, "*opening the gate*." I was rescued by my cell phone vibrating and humming, and then the screen lit up. My love wanted to know if I wanted to do some shopping with her. I typed back that I was on my way and closed off all other thoughts.

That was easier said than done, it was almost unnatural, but I only thought about the round up and the groceries and walked out the door. The village was small and I felt triumphant; I had silenced the voice for the second time. I chuckled that I had thought that in my own inner voice and that almost made me feel like a little child hopping over the pavement. Or, had it been allowed to me and who had then allowed it?

Some leaves were blowing by and a gust of wind passed me and I walked on with my head bowed in the wind that surrounded me and chilled me to the bone. When I reached the curb, I looked up and got the shock of my life. Less than a meter from me, a woman's face hovered at eye level, looking intently at me. It was dark black and had something of how I would have imagined a witch would look like, if I had any representation of what a witch would have looked like. "I am dreaming," I thought, "when I open my eyes I'll be in bed."

Then the big shock came, along the contours of the face I saw trucks that were for sale and I knew that I was well awake. "Oh," I moaned in fear and the face faded for a moment and then came back much sharper. I couldn't think anymore, I thought 'freezebrain' and I stepped off the sidewalk. A loud honking made me jump back on the curb and only a short resounding drum beat reminded me of what had just happened.

"You are hallucinating," I thought in my gravel voice. "Oh dear, I was thinking in my gravel voice again," I had been found again, "and the gross, rough voice laughed for a moment," *had you actually doubted that,* " it wanted to know.

I was seen or was being watched or constantly observed. As if I could get away from something that had been inside of me or was optionally inside of me or at least chased me. The face had really upset me beyond belief, you don't expect anything like that. It was gone after I had almost been run over. Now I saw all the trucks on the other side and that was a familiar sight. It had hovered at eye level and had filled me with deep fear and horror.

I looked left and then right and crossed carefully. "Hey partner," it sounded next to me and a heavy hand rested on my shoulder for a moment. I looked up and it was an old cowboy who had started walking up with me. "You were almost a goner, buddy," he laughed. "Be careful, there is more traffic than before." I chuckled, the man even rode to the cowboy church on his horse. I knew him from the Roundup.

"Oh, you know Ross," I said, "sometimes you walk deep in thought and you don't hear cars anymore, they have become electric and that is pretty dangerous." "Yep," he said, "a horse is always better." "Where is your horse," I asked, I was not used to seeing the old cowpoke walking.

"In the stable, with some hay," he replied, "new times hey, you can no longer tie your horse down in the center." "That would not be good," I thought, there is a lot of traffic and honking and you don't want your horse to panic. "No, you are darn right" Ross said, "I have seen it in the spring parade with Doug." "Oh," I said, did his horse run wild? "Well, not his horse," Ross grinned, "he had tried to train a Buffalo, he breeds buffalos, you know that, don't you." I didn't know that, but still nodded. "Of course that attracts attention," the old man continued,"and Doug likes that."

"He'd been training him for months, and it was always going well, he was going around the village, taking his hat off when he saw ladies, and then saying," *howdy m'am,* like a right gentleman. It goes well, as long as it goes well and it went well until the day of the parade when the band started playing, a shrill trumpet blast and some rolling of the drums and the poor beast went wild. ' I had not heard this before, which made sense because Doug always had coffee in the Roundup and people would not discuss that in his presence of course.

"So," I asked ..? "Old Buffie," snarled and scraped his hoof, "said the cowboy," and began work forward, straight through the brass band. He wanted to get away from the sound and knocked over drummers and tuba blowers and could no longer be sustained, the more people screamed the wilder old Buffie became. The crowd moved apart for the beast that now clearly went mad and ran towards houses. Doug was still on top of it as if he had ended up in a rodeo, he shouted **whoa boy**, but it didn't help any. Buffie plowed through garden gates, such an animal easily weighs 2000 pounds, and came to a standstill in a large garden after he had crushed numerous fencing. He lowered his head and started to graze. "

"How did it end," I asked while we were almost at the Roundup. "Oh," Ross said, "Doug has plenty of money, he had to pay for the damage and did so without complaining, and they tightened the rules a little." "What do you mean tighened," I wanted to know. "Only horses when animals walk along, things like that," Ross said.

Talking about Buffie we had come to the old building. "There you are," the gravel voice sounded, and to my dismay I saw the dark face hovering slightly above the roof, it looked at me with eyes narrowed. I froze in the middle of a step. "Hey partner," Ross said, "what have you got?"

"Do you see anything there, I asked and I pointed to the roof." Ross glanced up, "not that I can say that I see something, what did you see," he wanted to know? "A raven or something," I lied, just to say something. "Hmm," bad sign, "Ross thought," a *raven in the air, death and scare.* " He held the door open, "Cowboy wisdom," he laughed and walked towards the coffee table.

"Coffee," asked the girl who immediately came forward with the jug. "Please," I answered, and followed Ross to the coffee table where the old cowboys were seated. "Good morning, gentlemen," I said as I sat down a friendly but humble murmur greetd me. "San was almost done for," Ross said, just to say something, I assumed. "What do you mean," Sony asked, arranging his stetson. "Almost run over at the Ford dealer," the cowpoke replied, passing me the girl's coffee. "Too much traffic today," an old timer added beside me.

"He was almost squashed by a black car, like one from the 1950s, the sort you barely see anymore," Ross continued. All of a sudden I got the nasty feeling that the floating female face had lured me from the pavement to kill me. I pushed that thought away, but somewhere far away in my head I heard a rough chuckle. "I just wasn't paying attention," I explained, "and was able to jump away just in time." "It happens every day," said the old timer next to me, "two Indians near the thrift shop left us for the eternal hunting grounds, one speared and one spread out under the front wheel of a truck."

"Tell me," his neighbor said, "I was standing next to the store, it wasn't a pretty sight." "You saw it happening," I asked? "Certainly," the man answered. "It was old Rock, the grandson of Little Bighorn." "Little Bighorn," I asked, "and that's ...". "The chief and shaman of the Assiniboine tribe, he is two in one and enjoys a lot of respect among the local tribes," laughed the man, "everyone knows that and recognizes him" "I was looking at some tools and saw how old Rock came out with a package under his arm.

He seemed very excited and took out his cell phone and started phoning. " "Haha," said Ross, "no more smoke signals for the Assiniboine." "No," Sony replied, "only we white people have a motto under the municipal coat of arms that honors traditions." "... and that is," I asked? "*Where the past is the present*," it sounded from a few sides. "*Where the past is the present ...*" I asked in surprise, "meaning?" "Just that," said the girl who arrived with the coffee pot, "another refill?" We held out our mugs and the brown steaming moisture filled the mug to the rim. "Simple," she said again, as if she had to explain something to a stupid boy who was too thick to understand anything.

"The past and the present always touch each other, one comes from the other, and the present refers to what lies behind us. They are just dots in time that come together or move away. " My mouth almost opened, this was like the intersection story in the cave. "Gee," I said, "what a special motto. "The first pioneers took it from an Indian tribe," the girl said, walking on. "Another refill," she asked at the next table. The neighbor of the oldtimer blew over his mug for a moment and then carefully took a sip. He rinsed it in his mouth and swallowed it.

"So he was right excited and calling someone," he picked up the thread again, "and a little later the old Chevy from Little Bighorn appeared. The old gas guzzler stopped next to the sidewalk where old Rock stood who gave him the package through the window. Then the old musclecar raced away and disappeared from sight in no time. "That was it," Sony wanted to know? "Well, no," said the old man, "then old Rock crossed and a lumber truck came roaring around the corner and tried to brake with all its might, but old Rock came under the front wheel and was scraped over the road."

"Good God," said a cowpoke with eggs and bacon in front of him, " I am having a bite to eat, can you simmer down a bit .. boy what a story." "To make matters worse," the first speaker continued undisturbed, "an Indian on a motorbike hit the back of the truck, he probably tried to brake because the poor guy was launched and ended up speared on a tree trunk. " "Okay," the breakfasting cowboy said, "thank you, that will do," and he pushed his plate away.

"Gee," Sony said, "you see, if Little Bighorn had arrived a little later, Old Rock would have lived, and the truck would not have needed to brake, and the motorcyclist would have just come home." Yup, "Ross said," the past is the present ... things simply go the way they do. " Somehow far away in my mind I knew that it could never have happened otherwise, the bowl or some rotten demon had taken care of the brothers.

"Something different, Ross said," San just saw above the Roundup a big black raven. " "*Ravens around*," Sony said before him, "*dead in the ground*." I shivered. "Cowboy wisdom," said the old timer, "ravens always announce death." "Are you ready to go," sounded the voice of my love, who had come to stand next to the table. "Gentlemen," I said, my duty calls me to my shopping, see you tomorrow. " "Be seeing you," it sounded, and I followed my wife outside.

"You are quiet today," my wife said, while we drove to the Transcanada highway in the Chrysler and I knew she was right. I had half expected a flight of ravens or the dark woman's face or an admonishing gravel voice, but none of that happened. "Well, I am a bit lost in thought," was my reply, and I realized that I did not want to make her part of Indian chiefs and demons and bright blue-lit cellars. Because where would I start?

The radio wailed country western and I recognized an old one from Hank Williams; "*why must I love the heartless one*." It turned out to have been Jim Reeves, at least the announcer said that Jim was still very much missed, but it was and remained a tear jerker. Hank probably also released it or vice versa.

"You know how your dreams evaporate when you awake," my wife asked. I nodded and then said "yes," because I realized that she would not look sideways when she was driving. "My dream has not evaporated with me," she said, "it is constantly bugging me." "What do you mean," I asked, thinking I knew what it was about, but I wanted her to say it.

"From the lake where I was pulled away from the shore," she said. "How is it bugging you," I wanted to know? "Facets are coming back," she explained as she put the car on cruise control, "meaning that the car would automatically drive to Medicine Hat at the same speed. "There was a rolling drum sound," she continued, "but nothing that you would normally hear, it seemed arhythmic." "I also had drums in my dream," I said, but apparently she had not heard me because she just kept talking.

The Chrysler hovered over the TransCanada and my love only had to make slight steering adjustments. "There was an elevation above the shoreline," she said, "and somewhere in there was an opening, an opening from which light was shining, as if an old flash photo was being taken." I shivered involuntarily. "Just a flash," I asked. "No," she replied, "it had that fierceness and that light did not extinguish what you would have had with an old flash block."

The radio now spit out the 'fugitive'. "*After every road there is always one more city.*" *Down every road there is always one more city I'm on the run, the highway is my home I raise a lot or cane back in my younger days While Mama used to pray my crops would fail I'm a hunted fugitive with just two ways: Outrun the law or spend my life in jail I'd like to settle down but they won't let me A fugitive must be a rolling stone Down every road there is always one more city I'm on the run, the highway is my home ...*

I did have an image with that text, I felt that I was being followed or lived every day. My love turned off the radio. "It was a bright blue light," my sweetie said, "as bright as you would not expect. It caught my eye even though I was pulled away from the shoreline by a strong current. " I let that sink in for a moment. "That must have been special," I finally said, "if your life is at risk and you perceive something in the distance that has nothing to do with your problem, that is special."

"Hmm," she said, "and there's more, a figure with outstretched arms appeared in the opening." "I'm listening," I simply replied. "There is nothing more to say," she said earnestly, "I was pulled under and I only succeeded in re-emerging using every bit of strength I had in me."

We drove on in silence and when we arrived in Medicine Hat, she asked if I would like to have a snack and a coffee first at 'Original Joe's'. It was one of my favorite places and I immediately agreed. Medicine Hat was a big place and we even had to wait at some traffic lights, something you didn't have in our village. We finally drove into the large parking lot and stopped at what had become our favorite restaurant. A little later we were waiting to be brought to a table. The waitress approached us and smiled kindly. We knew the girl from the weeks we had been shopping in the Hat and she greeted us, in a genuine friendly way.

"What is the special today," I asked when we had a steaming cup of coffee in front of us. "Pulled pork, with Ceasar's salad," she told us. "That sounds great," I chuckled, no one serves pulled pork like Joe's. "You as well," the girl turned to my sweetie? "That would be too much," replied my dear, still with a severe drumming in her head. "Do me a Poutine, please." The girl froliced away and I announced that I would go to the washroom to freshen up. I looked in the mirror while I ran the tap to wash my hands.

I was satisfied with what I saw, I didn't look distinguished but well cared for. The water started to flow more and more slowly and eventually the tap dripped a little and then nothing came out anymore. I leaned forward, not understanding why the tap was open without water coming out. A soft gurgling sound echoed from the tap. I stooped a bit more and received a huge shock when I heard voices from the tap. Squeezed votes but clear enough to make them out. "*Get the bowl you retard*," it sounded half screaming. Another voice cut right through it, "*You want us to jerk your guts out, numb brain, get the bowl*." After that there was only crazy laughter. "*Why don't you listen to good advice,*" the gravel voice in my asked, while I was clinging to the sink not to fall over. "Why are you in my head," I asked? "*Because I needed a body,*" the rough gravel voice sounded, and a soft drumming rumble began somewhere between my ears.

I refound my balance and looked at the tap in disbelief. It first started to drip and then slowly to flow normally again. Yet I no longer felt the urge to hold my hands under that particular tap. I chose a sink that was far removed from the 'voices sink.' In the mirror I saw that I looked pale with big frightend eyes. I forced myself to hum and, as if it were a mantra, I managed to blank my mind. I walked to the air dryer and before I walked back to the restaurant I took a last look in the mirror and to my satisfaction I was myself again.

"The food has just been brought," my sweetheart said, and I was delighted to look at my pulled pork plate. The restaurant was rectangular in shape and a mega-screen hung on every wall. Your eye was drawn to it unintentionally. There was a rerun of the Antiques roadshow and while enjoying the delicious pulled pork I followed it with half an eye. "You might think," the expert said, "it's just an old bottle, but what would you say if I told you it was 13th century?" "Goodness me," exclaimed the old bent woman, "from the year thirteen hundred?" "No," said the smartly dressed gentleman with the bow tie, "older, the 13th century began 1 day after the year 1200." "Yes, yes," the female muttered, "and you can see that?" "With certainty," the expert smiled, he arranged his bow tie," the glass is impure, "he continued and held it up to the light and slowly turned the bottle between his fingers. "It comes from the Venetian workshops," he said thoughtfully, "the color, tells it all."

He placed a monocle before his right eye and looked at the object with even more attention. "Wood-burning furnaces do that," he said, "the Venetians imported raw materials such as glass chunks and enamels, in this case I suspect trace elements of lead." The old lady was listening breathlessly and I just remembered that I shouldn't let my pulled pork get cold and my fork found the way back to my plate. "Hmm," said the bow tie expert, "reminds me of Angelo Salerno's work, but that would have been more sophisticated."

"Gee', my dear said, 'from the thirteenth century, that such a thing is not broken. " These were wonderful moments, simply without worries about demonic bowls that are compellingly trying to control your life. "What would it be worth," my sweetie asked me. "I had no idea and said," What a fool gives for it, but it's old and that will certainly count. " "$ 35,000," said the roadshow expert, "whenever you want to, you can auction it, old glass and specifically the early Venetian, has its value." "Oooh," the old lady screamed and put her hand over her mouth. 'Who would have thought that'! "Would you sell it," my dear asked? "If I needed the money," I replied, "but it is also special to have something from the year 1200 or so."

The camera now went to an art expert who was admiring a painting with great attention. "Typical image," said the man, "early Christian Pilate's work." The man who had brought in the piece looked silently at the expert. "What does that mean," he finally asked. "Pontius Pilate, condemned Christ to the cross," said the expert, in haughty voice, "but he realized that Christ was innocent, and washed his hands in a bowl because he did not want the blood of Jesus on him."

The camera now zoomed in on Pontius' hands and the bowl that caught the water that the servant was pouring out over his master's hands. My fork froze in midair. The bowl was enlarged and enlarged and I saw what my love saw. She looked at me in dismay, "that is..," she said, and I finished..'looks like..'

"*Looks like,*" the gravel voice sounded in my head, "looks like?" A rough laugh echoed and a drum beat sounded between my ears. "*The anti Holy Grail,*" the voice mocked, and was followed finally by two more drum beats.

We finished our plates in silence while another expert was being consulted about a spinning wheel. I put down the money we owed and a tip for the waitress, waved at the girl behind the bar and we walked back to the Chrysler. "It bore a striking resemblance to our bowl," my sweetie said, as she started the heavy v8. "It was early Christian art, according to that expert," I said, "so it probably didn't really reflect how things had been, it was more of an impression." I thought of the demonic voice that had sounded from the tap and that had promised to tear my guts out. " "Besides," I added, "there would have been no clay bowl in the household of Pontius Pilate."

The man represented the supreme authority of the Roman empire in Israel. You would rather have expected a golden or silver bowl. " It might have been a coincidence, "my wife explained," but it looked a lot like the bowl that I chugged away. "

She turned the car into a spacious parking spot and a moment later we walked to Sobeys, which made Walmart look like a Micky mouse supermarket in size. Supermarkets in North America really deserve the name supermarkets.

Everything was there that you could wish for, the land of milk and honey, I thought, the land where there were no shortages! I was still pondering the bowl in my head, while my wife was busy weighing freshly flown in strawberries, I said, "That bowl certainly gave me a bad feeling and you couldn't take a photo of it and send it on." My wife gave me a piercing look and said, "That's why I threw it away. The bowl made me gloomy and frightened me. It is probably in pieces in the garbage dump by now. "

She closed the bag with the strawberries and stuck a price label on it that had just printed out. At the cashout the boy looked at the groceries and said 'that will be $280, you can pick up a free turkey from the freezer.' 'A free turkey', I asked? 'Any bill above $250, gets a free turkey,' the boy smiled. 'Well I'll be ..' I laughed and selected a big bird.

It was cold outside as I wheeled the trolley to the car. I started loading the shoppings in the trunk of the big American, and froze when the turkey spoke to me. *'Get the bloody bowl, you idot,'* the voice had come from the deep frozen bird, and I almost dropped te bags with fruits.

In the car the love my life again stated who nice it was that the bowl was on the dump in a trillion pieces.

"Actually it's not there," I reported. "And you know that," my wife asked in surprise? I think I know, "I explained," it's a long story, but one of the men from the Roundup saw how old Rock was knocked down and how he had just given a package to little Bighorn. " Who may that be that Rock and that Bighorn, 'my love asked and she looked at me almost reproachfully as if I had with held information and as a matter of fact I had done just that. "The man's real name is Old Rock," I began, "or I should say, was called Old Rock and he was the grandson of Little Bighorn."

"Right," my wife said, "and who is that Bighorn?" "Let's go to the coffee corner," I suggested, "then we can catch up." The girl with the coffee pot came by and filled our mugs and I must have looked confused. Where to start?

"So much has happened," I said, "let me start with the bowl that you threw away. It was indeed gone, but when I spoke to the neighbor, the day I sawed the tree in bits that had fallen over, he told me that he had chased away two Indians who were looking for bottles in the bins " " Yes,' said my wife, who gave me full attention. "They took the bowl," I explained. "The neighbor also told me about the previous occupants of our house, there were three of them. They all died in bad ways. " "A day later," my dear said, "the neighbor broke his neck and he too was dead." I nodded. "That's right," I agreed. "The last two went crazy," I said, "they thought they heard voices and died in unpleasant ways." "What do you think," my sweetheart asked urgently. "I don't exclude it, you know the hearing of voices," I said honestly, "perhaps in their heads, but it's not unthinkable."

"I saw Old Rock lying under the truck. He was dead and his brother was speared on a tree trunk. He had run into the back of the lumber truck with his bike. It was not a pleasant sight and I went into the Thriftstore and there Les gave me a cup of tea because I was about to faint. He told me that the dead Indian under the wheel had just bought a bowl. I assume it was our bowl. " "I wish," my wife said emphatically, "that you would not call it *our* bowl." The man in the roundup saw Old Rock coming out and he gave a package, I take it to have been the bowl, to a man in a car and that was little Bighorn. He had phoned him, "I added.

"Let me get this straight," my dear said, and suddenly she looked tired and serious. Three previous owners died. The neighbor who told you that, died as well. Two Indians who had to deal with the bowl died. Les has had a stroke and died, the bowl was in his shop for only a short while. That's 7 people and that bowl was called a **blessing** bowl! "

"Now I would like to know," she concluded, "who that Bighorn is." His name is actually Little Bighorn, I corrected her, "and he is the chief and shaman of the Assiniboine tribe, he is two in one and enjoys great respect among the local tribes." "And how do you know all this," she asked?

"From the roundup men," I answered. "We are sleeping poorly," my dear said, "and you have nightmares and my dreams stay with me, seven people died and I cannot help but feel that it is because of that damned dish, or at least it has to do with it. I am not interested in whether it is the Pilates bowl or an old possessed bowl, I am glad it is out of my house. "I don't want to hear anything more about it," she continued, "it gives me the shivers, come on we will finish the shopping list and have a nice day."

But I knew that if I didn't find the bowl, my guts would be torn out, that had not been a promise, but a shouted threat from an unholy voice from a washroom tap, and I wasn't waiting for that to happen. No matter how it was intended, I took it very seriously, the image of the smeared out Indian came to my mind again, the owner of the voice meant business and I resolved that, no matter how, I had to get that bowl back.

.-&-.

My sweetheart pressed on cruise control and, just like everyone else, we drove away from Medicine Hat. "Nice gesture from that turkey," my sweetie said, and I thought, "you should know what a scary thing it is." "That you get such a beast for free," she continued. "Yes," I agreed, "that's quite something." I did not want that beast in my house, I resolved, not after it had spoken to me.

"I'm not so fond of turkey," I began, "and it was free so I am not too sure about the quality." "We will never finish together," my dear agreed. "Would you mind if I gave it to my sister as a gift," I asked, "she always has people from the church over the floor." "No," my sweetie answered. "Then at least that beast has served a purpose." "Nice," I thought, "I've dumped it and I can immediately see my sister."

It was a relaxed ride along the prairie, everyone kept to the speed limit and as a long colored train we all drove on cruise control towards the East. Next to us a real train came by, there was no end to it, like all trains in the prairie states they are not meant for passenger transport. It is mainly grain wagons that go to the large silos. The train was clearly faster than we were and we saw it later in the distance against a slope.

A tunnel started at the head and a communication mast at the tail. My love set the day counter to zero when we arrived at the mast and told me when we were aware of the tunnel, "I can't believe it, that train was approximately one kilometer long." "We don't give away turkeys in Europe," I smiled, "nor do we have trains of a kilometer in length." "And unfortunately we have a blessing bowl here," I thought, but I did not say it. The state border was marked by the provincial flag of Saskatchewan.

The corn stalks were of course represented in the flag. A herd of bisons along the side of the road looked at us in surprise, as if they had never seen cars and gazelles were grazing in the distance, a moment later we arrived at the exit for our village. I left that unholy turkey in the trunk and when the rest of the groceries had been cleared, I took over the keys from my love and headed for my sister. She was happy to see me and she had Father Peter visiting with two elders, one of the elders had half Indian characteristics. A Bible lay open and I asked, "I am not disturbing," realizing that of course I was.

My sister gave me a kiss and said, "No, silly boy, we are just about to have some tea, would you like a cup too?" "Blessed are those invited to the table of the Lord," said the Indian elder. "And *he* is here," I asked, and I kept the rest I wanted to say to myself because my sister gave me a dark look. "Where two are united in his name," the Indian said piously, pointing to the open Bible, "the Lord is in their midst."

"Right," I said, "it always feels good to be welcome." "Are you coming for the Bible study," Father Peter asked, whom I had always liked. "No, father," I answered truthfully, "I came by to give my sister a turkey and ask for some things. "That's nice," said the priest, "it's nice to think of your sister." I nodded. "I'll get the turkey out of the car before it thaws out," I said. "Then I'll pour the tea," my sister said.

When I arrived at the car, I shoved the unholy bird into a shopping bag and walked to the door, half and half expecting a warning voice to sound from the bag, but the turkey had already expressed its message and I would not forget it. There was a cup of tea in front of an empty chair and I sat down at the table. My sister took the shopping bag and said, "That's a good-sized one."

"What did you want to know," she asked when we were all having tea, "something about the village?" "Maybe so," I replied, "could it be that Jewish attributes ended up here in the village, relics or something." Father Peter looked at me thoughtfully for a moment, "not specifically Jewish, let's say about their religion or culture, but some attributes that had to do with their former country."

I did not want to seem eager and first took a sip of tea. "What do you mean father," I asked? "Where the library is now," said the man of God, "was first an early Christian congregation. It was a coptic church. In our church, in the side nave, a piece of old stained glass has been placed that has been donated by them. " The side chapel is no longer really used, except for baptisms. " "Father," I asked,

"I am not so informed in churches and all, what should I imagine from Coptic church?"

Father Peter gave me a friendly look, "I'll enlighten you," he laughed. "The word kop is an Arabic corruption of the Greek word for Egypt: Ægyptos, originally *Hoet-ka-Ptah* (home of the ka of Ptah), the name of the great Ptah temple in ancient Memphis, the city of Ptah." "Right," I said, but I didn't know anything yet. The priest's eyes glistened, he clearly came to his hobby horse church history. 'For the Copts the' Flight of the Holy Family to Egypt 'is, Joseph and Mary and the baby Jesus, of great importance and according to them the holy family has been in Egypt with the midwife Salome for three and a half years. According to Saint Luke, Egyptians were present at Pentecost and established Christian communities in the year 33 when they were back in Egypt.

According to tradition, the Christianization was done by Marcus. Marcus established the "seat of Alexandria" and became a martyr there on 8 May in the year 68. With a rope around his neck, he was dragged through the streets until he died. His body was buried in the church of St. Mark in Bucolia. In 828 his body was taken by the Venetians, but his head remained in Alexandria. "

"So there is an Egyptian Christian church," I asked in disbelief, I had always assumed that Egypt was a Muslim. "Ha ha is there a Christian church," the priest said full of fire, probably older than Rome, she has about 11 million believers in Egypt. "Amen, the Lord be praised," said the two elders almost simultaneously. "That church had fewer and fewer followers and finally had to close, father Peter continued.

They were also very much out of touch with the community. The men in turban and the women in black, gloomy clothes. "So the few remaining members went to the churches with their sacred treasures and gave them to their Christian brothers before closing their church. We received the fire-painted piece of window. I just said that the head of St Mark's head would have remained in Alexandria. " "Yes," I agreed, the priest had said so."Copts have that a bit," smiled the man of God, "they turn a body part into a relic. We could have gotten a finger from Paulus de Hermite, also known as Paulus from Thebes, but I really didn't like the idea. The Lutherans now have that, as I understand it. So we took the piece of window and some pottery. " I was suddenly full of attention. "Father," I asked, "what is depicted on the piece of window?" "The damnation and the first indulgence of guilt," said Peter. "I don't follow you, father," I said, "what does that mean?"

"Pontius Pilate who washed his hands in innocence," said the Anglican priest. "Good grace," I exclaimed, 'Pontius Pilate!' "Yes," said the priest, and the pottery completed the still life. "What kind of pottery," I asked while I could barely control myself. "Symbolically, I suppose," said Peter, "a jug was placed on a table in front of the window and a bowl to wash your hands in." It was as if lightning struck me. "And that was brought by ..." I asked? "The last two nuns of that church," said the Lord's servant, "then the demolition company came and later the library was built."

My head was spinning and puzzle pieces just fell into place. "Sweet Brother would you like some more tea," my sister asked again with more emphasis and I realized that she had already asked. "Excuse me," I said, " I was lost in thought, just a little sip," and I held out my mug. I looked at the Indian elder, "what can you tell me about Little Big Horn?" "I am a Christian," said the man, "I am no longer in the Shaman, and this is a Christian gathering," and he crossed himself.

I emptied my mug and looked at Father Peter, 'thank you for your explanation, it was very enlightening. I kissed my sister, waved half to the two elders, and walked to the front door. Tomorrow I would pick an Indian in the Jasper's where they always gambled and drank. I had the idea that I had taken 7 miles with 1 step. I knew the feeling, I had taken control of the situation. " *You really think so,*" asked the raw gravel voice between my ears.

"How was it at your sister's," my sweetheart asked as I stepped into our house. "Nice," I replied, "Father Peter was there with two elders." "That was nice," my wife asked? "Yes, it was," I laughed, "father Peter is a fine person and one of the elders was an Indian, but he was more Christian than anyone else." I doubted whether or not I would tell her about the Pilate bowl and decided to do it, otherwise you end up walking around with more and more secrets.

"Father Peter," I began, "told me about how there as once a Coptic church here in the village. I had never heard of that, so I asked what I should picture by that and it turns out to to have been an early Christian church in Egypt, older than the church of Rome. " Christianity in Egypt, "my wife asked surprised? "I thought it was sort of special as well," I admitted. "With the infanticide in Bethlehem commissioned by King Herod, Mary and Joseph escaped with the baby Jesus by going to Egypt. Only a few years later did they return to their own country. "

"I knew nothing about that," my wife said. "It's apparently in the Bible," I continued, "and the Indian elder might find it for you in split seconds." My love took her tablet and typed something in. "Gee," she exclaimed, "you can find it immediately, isn't Google wonderful." "What does it say," I asked?

"The flight to Egypt," she read, "is the story in Matthew 2: 13-23 about the flight of Joseph and Mary with the newborn baby Jesus to Egypt after they were warned about the upcoming infanticide in Bethlehem."

"In Egypt there is a large number of churches and shrines of the Coptic church in places where, according to tradition, the holy family stayed. The most important of these churches is Abu Sarga, a 4th-century church in Cairo. " "Father Peter who knows a lot about historical history," I added, "was able to tell me that the Coptic Church has 11 million members." "That's a fair number," my dear agreed. "There is more," she said, "just listen." "The story in Matthew The story about the flight to Egypt appears only in Matthew. This gospel relates that the sages from the East were looking for the newborn "king of the Jews." King Herod heard of this and ordered his soldiers to go to Bethlehem and kill all the boys up to two years old (the child murder of Bethlehem. However, an angel appeared to Joseph in a dream and told him to flee to Egypt with Jesus and Mary. "

"What a terrible story," I thought, "that those soldiers obeyed their king, some must have had children of their own." "The Bible is full of that kind of misery," my wife said. "That poor woman," she went on, "she had just given birth under terrible conditions, in a stable, and then had to flee with her newborn baby in her arms." "Yes," I said, "they certainly had a tough start." "And, finely," I continued, "there was a Coptic church in our village, that church was suffering, cowboys did not feel too connected to prayers wailing people in long robes. The women had taken their old habits with them and walked around veiled, and the church declined in numbers per year. " "I have a picture with that," my wife confirmed, "no one likes that, it would have been wise if they had adjusted more."

"After a while the church was to be dissolved, Father Peter said," I continued, "and the townhall had put its eyes on that place to build the library that is now there. The church was sold and demolished and the land fell to the municipality. " "What a trouble for those people," my wife said, "you come with your church all the way from Egypt and you can't find an audience." I nodded but I understood, "there are a lot of traditional churches here," I said, "and then you don't have a need to join a church that is Christian but has different rites. "

"That was it," my sweetie asked, "because you were gone a long time?" "No I answered truthfully," before the church was closed, they distributed their shrines amongst their brother Christians. My wife looked questioningly at me. "Our church received a piece of old glass that is now placed in the side chapel." The Lutheran church wanted a bit of a finger of the holy hermit of Thebes. " "How horrid," my love cried, "who would want that?"

"There was something else that our church received," I continued, "an old table with an old clay bowl on it." My life long companion jumped up and was all attention, "and," she wanted to know, "and is it what I think it is?" It was a tableaux vivant that went with the piece of glass, "I said slowly, weighing every word," and do you want to know what was depicted on the piece of glass? " "Yes," she said, leaning forward. "Pontius Pilate washing his hands in innocence," I said softly. "Almighty," she exclaimed, putting her hand to her mouth, "would it be true, would that bowl have come all the way from the Middle East?" "I suspect that might be the case," I said, "and I felt a shiver run down my back. *"Now you have shared it with the woman*," said the raw gravel voice, "*now she is involved, will you man folk learn nothing at all, but nothing at all from the past?"*

"You know," my wife said, "I don't care where the cursed thing came from, I thought it was a nasty bowl, and whether it came from the Middle East or not, I'm glad it is gone from my house." I thought about my guts. The voice from the tap had 'promised' me that they would be pulled out if I didn't get hold of the bowl and I just had the idea that it wasn't an empty threat. Without wanting to do it, I had become pivotal in a demonic game.

I had become the owner, together with my wife, of a house that had a cellar that could be called very very different indeed. "That was just a dream," I told myself. "*And you want to believe that*," a raw voice sounded between my ears, accompanied by a drum beat. And I knew it didn't make sense to fool myself.

The first dream had been one about a plain on which I walked and a cave in the distance and the enormous loneliness I had experienced. After that everything went fast, sounds from the cellar, drumming on bongos, voices that spoke to me from objects.

Occasionally my hand was directed against my will and I had emptied my coffee against my will, in fact I had tried to resist, my wrist had simply been turned around. The story of the deceased previous owners had just been told by my neighbor or he found his end by plunging down a ladder. If that wasn't enough, two Indians who had probably taken the bowl out of my garbage bin had died and the nice owner of the Thrift store, where the bowl had landed, had suffered a stroke.

My inner voice changed from time to time or was accompanied by a raw gravel voice and if I didn't know better then as an outsider I would think that I was going crazy. My 'case' would fill entire symposia of psychiatrists if they only half knew what was happening to me. The rumble had moved with me to my sister's house when I went to drink a cup of tea there and I had called on her not to open the hatch of her cellar because there was something unholy down there lying in wait. It was clear I was the pivot. The bowl had been given to me and I was the co-owner of the house. Everything related to it, followed me and apparently time was running out.

The demon in me had told me that he had needed a body and had therefore entered my head. I was also told that there were intersections in time and that the time was ripe because all was ligning up. Poor me, I didn't know what to do or what was expected of me. But I knew with deep conviction that if I did not live up to the expectation of all that persecuted me, I would be the fourth deceased owner of this house. I wondered if the previous owners had also not met their 'obligations'. Then why did my neighbor die?

I just thought he had said too much, he had been the one who told me about the three previous owners and the strange ways in which they had died. How would my guts be torn out? Surely that was not possible. For a moment I became dizzy and I saw myself lying in a flash on a deserted plain, close to a cave opening in a rock wall and I was shocked because there were ravens on me that were feasting on me. I shook it off and thought of my cellar where the workplace radiated blue light and where the voice of my deceased neighbor had asked me to put the bowl on a 'point of intersection'.

I thought he had pointed out the place that emitted blinding light. "You are miles away," my wife said, "you've had that lately," a penny for your thoughts. "Oh well," I said, "I was indeed far away, so much has happened and I thought about the environment here and our house and that I would like to know more about the population, the Indian tribes and such."

"I was thinking," my wife said, "that if you can put the smoker on the concrete platform, I can smoke some spare ribs." That was the last place where I wanted to have my love, that was the place where the shed had been where the second owner died screeching his lungs out while he burnt to death.

"I'll put it by the kitchen door, close to the fire pit," I said, "then we don't have to walk too far and why don't we invite the neighbors, then I'll put some chairs and a table outside and later we can light a fire in the fire pit and enjoy a few drinks and disconnect from all the misery we have experienced in recent times. ' "How nice," my wife said. I'm going to call the neighbor's wife immediately. "

"That my young friend," the gravel voice sounded in my head, *"you did well.* "I'm not young," I protested, "and you're not my friend." "Ah," said the gravel voice, *"age is just a number, if you are a few thousand years old then you will find*

everyone young and as far as friendship is concerned, you cannot always pick out your friends and I have chosen you, that makes you one of my circle."

The smoker gave off a pleasant scent. The spare ribs had been roasting in the smoke for a few hours on the grills. Occasionally my love came out and filled the bottom of the tray with some herbs and pieces of wood. Half North America sits out in the garden with friends and neighbors at the first ray of sunshine, but always with a barbequeue or a smoker. The 'smoker' of meat takes many hours and also the necessary care, but the end result is worth it. The taste is what makes all the effort worthwhile. It would be a while before Barry and Clarene were to arrive and I wondered what I would do in the meantime. The garden was mowed and everything looked spic and span.

I had already laid branches in the outdoor firepit and some pine cones, in short the lazy chairs were around what would be a cozy campfire with side tables and I looked at everything with pleasure. The neighbors were hospitable people, they had been the owners of a supermarket and had sold everything a few years ago and had started to enjoy their early retirement. They had traveled a lot and Barry then went hunting a lot, really a lot. I had been surprised when I was invited to their home for the first time.

Everyone in Canada hunts or has hunted or has been on the hunt, the country lends itself to it and there is also a need for control. Otherwise, for example, the deer population would grow rampant and in the winter eat the bark of the trees and destroy entire forest. In addition, you have of course the cougars also known as the mountain lion who comes to the villages in times of scarcity to see what can be hunted.

Barry had shown me a cougar that was as big as a tiger. I realized that if you came across a cougar like that without a gun, you didn't stand a chance. I had never seen such a collection of stuffed animals as at his home. At first I had mixed feelings about the stuffed animals but behind every beast there was a story. The animals were not a trophy but more because my neighbor had measured his strength with them and respected the animal he had killed and he wanted to keep the memory tangible.

His wife did not like all those stuffed animals and in the end they were neatly arranged in a separate room and the living room became the living room where people did not think they were on a hunting expedition. That 'game room' had been large enough to house a bear, a Caribou, a Moose and any kind of beast that was simply large. It was clear to me that Barry had been a big game hunter.

"This bear is a grizzly bear," Barry had told me as we walked past his collection, and he looked with a thoughtful look. "Boy, that is a big one," I exclaimed. The animal had his teeth bared and his front paw raised, ready to strike. "We flew to Alaska," Barry said, "we did that with a pipercup." "Were you with a group of hunters," I asked? "No," Barry had replied, "I was with an Indian guide from here. A man who can almost smell tracks. We were dropped and the plane would return after exactly a week.

I always brought the same guide. That creates a bond in the 'bush' you are dependent on each other and then it is good if you know each other well. ' I nodded but had never experienced anything like it. 'You tell each other stories in the night before you go hunting. Life stories that stay in the 'bush' afterwards. "We walked around for days and only ate from the land," Barry continued. "After a while we arrived in an area that was utterly inhospitable. Old Rock suddenly stopped and glanced around. "We are in the area of the big bear," he had said. "He sniffed the air and turned to the mountains, that's where we have to go," he said. "I asked him if he knew for sure," Barry said, "and he had looked at me with pity. "Don't you feel the spirit of the bear," he had asked, almost surprised. "That's how they are," Barry continued, "they feel the animals before they see them.

I had looked at Barry and then at the bear and then at Barry again. He seemed to be in a trance. He was back in Alaska for a moment and stood next to an Indian who was called Old Rock and who could feel bears from a distance. "Anyway," he said suddenly, "it was a beautiful bear and here he is." It was clear I had not been there and did not share the moment he had experienced with the guide.

"What kind of gun do you have," I had just asked to say something. "Just single shot," my neighbor had replied. I probably looked surprised because he added, "I've never liked when hunters go into the bush with half machine guns. You compete you see, you measure your powers and your instincts. " "But if you miss your shot," I asked?

"Then you won't come home," my neighbor had answered laconically. "And the guide," I wanted to know. "Nothing," my neighbor had said, "a bowie knife, he doesn't believe in" thunder sticks. " I had heard all this and understood why Barry took the killed animals home. He had entered into a showdown and respected the opponent and did not want to leave the carcass to rot. "Very special," I thought, "you don't experience anything like that in Europe."

There was something, I knew there was something. I arranged the seats again and then it came to the fore. Barry had taken the guide from our village and he said he was called old Rock. It dawned on me with full force now, the grandson of Little Bighorn who had ended under a truck wheel was also called old Rock, that could not be a coincidence, it was unthinkable that two Indians were walking around in our village with the same name. Barry had hunted with him, often hunted with him, they had shared life stories. They had been dependent on each other at dangerous moments.

"Soon after dinner," I assumed, "when the fire is on and we have a glass of whiskey in my hand, I can start asking about Little Bighorn." My thoughts were roughly disturbed by my love who came out and asked me, "Do you want to do something for me." "Of course," I said. "Do you want to go to the store," she asked, "and get some herbs for me," I put them on a list. " A little later I drove to the supermarket with the rumbling American and the grizzly bear, Barry and the Indian had vanished, my assignment was to find the herbs that were on the list and to bring them back as quickly as possible.

There was a large raven perched above the supermarket entrance overlooking the parking area. I was convinced that the raven was waiting for me and I wondered if he would attack me if I left the car. "*Raven around dead in the ground,*" one of the old cowboys had said in the Round up, or something in that spirit. I started to accept that seriously, you can't just brush away cowboy wisdom. In any case, the cowboys had been convinced that raven were the messengers of death.

I exhorted myself and got out, it was difficult for me to come home with a story that I had not entered the store because there was a bird above the entrance. With my head retracted, I walked towards the store and I arrived at the same time as a couple, pushing a shopping cart to the sliding doors. The raven looked down at us and fluttered once with his wings and uttered a chilling scream. My heart skipped and I more or less expected the animal to throw itself on my neck. But none of that happened and a moment later I stood among the aisles with herbs. Too quickly to my liking I finished the list and went to the cash register, I held only a few pots in my hand and joined the queue that was waiting.

The girl made a remark here or there, and without hurrying, the line kept moving forward. I looked past the shoppers at the parking lot and saw my car standing next to the lamppost. A large huddled dark shape was waiting on top of the lamp holder. I forced myself to focus on the cash register. "*Ravens around ...*" it sang in my head and without wanting, "I supplemented it," *dead in the ground*. The line moved on and I looked again at the parking lot. There was the raven that oversaw everything, the bringer of deathly tidings, still on the lamppost. "Who was dead in the ground," I wondered, "was that me," or was I to become the dead man in the ground. I shook the thought off, but you cannot always get rid of nasty thoughts that easily.

"Would you consider the basement also as under the ground," or was I carrying it too far, "and had birds not been the carriers of souls in mythology." I started to become obsessed, I realized, I focused on the jars in my hand and moved a little more towards the assistant behind the counter. "I hope they won't sit down on my shed later," I thought. I put the jars on the belt and they came right to the the scanning machine that always lit up with a red glow. I looked up in shock by a hard blow to the window.

A large black shape rose from the ground and shook its feathers for a moment and chose for the sky again, then disappeared from sight. "That flew full force against the window," the girl said in surprise, "you don't see that every day. "He was looking for something," said an old cowboy behind me with a cart full of steaks. " "*He was looking for someone,*" the gravel voice rang between my ears. I don't need to know, I told myself, birds flying against windows is a well-known fact. "But you were behind that window," my pestering demon.

spoke again with my rough inner voice. "That was quite a blast," I said to the girl as I paid up. "Boy," she said, "tell me something, I've never seen anything like it." The old cowboy briefly shifted his hat and then said, "Nothing happens for no reason." I didn't go into that because if something had been the reason, it would have been me, I was getting pretty sure of that.

She handed me the plastic shopping bag with the herbs and then said, 'have a nice day' and with that the raven had become a past event to her. "You too," I said, walking slowly toward the exit. I looked at the lamppost next to my car, but that was just an abandoned pole in a parking lot, yet I left the store with my neck pulled in.

The neighbors came and there was small talk and pleasantries. Everything was just fine and friendly and the smoker had done his job well and the food was delicious and in short you could say that it was a welcome change from all the problems, dreams, inner voices, deaths that had played such a role in my life of late. Barry and I lit the fire in the pit while the ladies removed the plates. "Barry," I asked, "are you a whiskey man?"

"It depends on the whiskey," he laughed, adjusting the chairs around the fire. *"Fireball,"* I replied, "a hearty *Saskatchewan bourbon."* "Only if you twist my arm," he chuckled. "Then you leave me no choice," I said, "if you watch over the fire, I'll get two glasses and the devilish bourbon." A little later we sat like if we had been friends for years and enjoyed every sip of 'fireball'. it would have been a perfect eve if not a nasty cry had disturbed the peace. I looked up in shock, then saw a dark shadow slide across the garden.

"There he is," said my neighbor, pointing his finger at my carport where a large raven had perched. It looked like the monster that had observed me at the supermarket. "Isn't that something," said Barry, "that was the totem animal of Old Rock, my guide who ended so poorly." "What do you mean," I asked, 'what is a totem animal? " Barry took a sip of fireball and rinsed it around in his mouth, "you know," he began, "when you're out in the bush waiting for your prey, you share your stories." I nodded he had told me that before.

"I had a very good relationship with Old Rock," he continued. "He told me a lot about his faith and background." This was a gift from God, I had wanted to talk to him about old Rock and now the raven had brought him up. He paused for a moment and then said, "The Old Rock totem animal was the raven, and when we hunted you always saw one that stayed close by, it may have been a coincidence, but I don't believe that." "I don't know what you mean by totem animal," I replied, filling our glasses up again. "The concept of totem animal comes from shamanism," my neighbor said slowly, formulating every sentence,

"a complex belief in the afterlife with eternal hunting grounds where the warrior is immortal and his deeds are accompanied by the drums of the great Spirit." I shivered when he toldme about the drumming.

"A totem animal is a spirit creature with an animal shape that has been assigned to a specific human being," Barry continued, taking a sip of whiskey. 'In essence, it is not necessarily an animal, although it does' show' itself in an animal form. The form in which this 'companion' shows itself says more about the qualities that the human being needs to support his 'earthly mission', than about the 'spirit being' that fulfills this function. " "I don't know if you think that's something to be laughed at," said my neighbor, "but it's what Old Rock and his people believe, in the thinking of shamanism, a totem animal is the animal assigned to a certain human as a protector, with the aim is for the person concerned to fulfill his 'mission' on earth. This means that a totem animal can also cause fears in humans if this is necessary to guide them back to their 'mission'. " "Boy," I thought, "tell me," I had only known fears since I had moved in.

"The totem is the" core of his strength "and a symbolic" embodiment "of his or her talents, a piece of soul capable of good or bad." "And you know these matter from hunting," I asked with interest? "Of the very many hunting parties I've shared with Old Rock," replied my neighbor, "at night, waiting for your prey, you expose your soul and share your fears and secrets." I nodded understandingly again but still had to process a lot.

"Do you know more about poor Old Rock's totem," I wanted to know as I took the bottle with a hand that shook a little. "Oh what shall I say," said Barry, "keeping up his glass," my guide had the raven as a totem animal, and his preferred color was blue. " The light in my basement had been a bright blue, and I realized that nothing but nothing happened with no reason in this world. He took a sip, then looked at the raven watching him with great attention. "There was more," he said, "his spiritual protector is the *Mudjekeewis.*" "I'm sorry that doesn't mean anything to me," I said honestly.

"Well," Barry sighed, "I get that, but all I remember is that Mudjekeewis is the firstborn son of the E-bangishimog, the Westwind, and is considered a guardian of tradition and ceremonies." "That's why he's here," said the neighbor in a voice that had a bourbon ring in it. "The Raven," I asked knowing the answer. "Yes," said Barry, "he's coming to say goodbye and he's leading someone or something back to the" mission. "

He was probably looking for me, "said the neighbor. But I thought, I'm the one he is looking for. "Let's wish him good things," said Barry, raising his glass to the raven. "Good friend, guide in perilous times," he said solemnly, "skim the hunting fields and be a free soul." "That's nice," I thought, but I noticed that the raven was now tilting his head and watching me closely.

"I raised my glass to the beast that might have been a totem or not, or something in my head or whatever, through whiskey mists I said as I spoke slowly and solemnly," I understand your mission oh Old Rock and it will be fulfilled. " The raven flapped its wings and disappeared into the twilight. "Here come the ladies," I said, "thank you for your explanation," and I thought, 'I bought some time'.

The fire slowly went out and the guests had left us a while back after a lovely evening and I sat with my love watching the glow of the fire under the stars. "We should go in," said my dear, and I nodded in agreement as I tried to shake off the slow lazy feeling and got up. I could have sat there forever, I had made a promise Old Rock's totem animal, and I was at peace with the world. The next day I would not have to go to the Jasper's lounge anymore, I knew what I wanted to know about Indians and their beliefs and hunting grounds,

I had just received that information from Barry. I decided to go to the reserve and see if I could somehow figure out where to find and lay my hands on the bowl. Maybe I could simply ask for Little big Horn or maybe it was wise to walk around first and then determine a course of action to follow. In any case, I knew that Little Big Horn had custody of the bowl, the cowboy in the roundup had said so, he had seen the bowl being handed to the medicineman by Old Rock.

He had the bowl and I had the crossroads in my basement. In addition, I had been promised what would happen to my guts if I didn't get the bowl back and I had no doubts about the truthfulness of that promise. In any case, I wanted to live my own life again with my own inner voice and with my intestines where they should be.

So we stepped into our bed tired but satisfied and a little later and I felt myself slipping into a slumber and I managed to stroke my sweetheart's hand before crashing backwards into a deep black night. I fell and slipped through layers of the night and floated until I lingered motionless. "Like the raven," was one of my last coherent thoughts, "praying on powerful wings, looking for prey." Suddenly my floating turned into a whimsical dive and I bounced back in my bed with my eyes wide open in my dark bedroom.

A soft rumble started under the bedroom and I knew what was happening there, a bright blue light would be shining there and the dark one would sneak up on me and force me to go to the opening. Deep within me I knew with certainty that if I did not obey the dark one I would be destroyed.

"*Are you done flying*," asked the raw gravel voice with feigned interest. "No," I thought, "not again, I made peace with the raven." "*You are a fool,*" said the gravel voice. "*The Raven does not rest until the sacrifice is made, and you are the chosen one.*" The drumming became a regular drum now, and I thought with horror at Barry's story about the drums of the great Spirit. "You know where you're going," the raw voice chuckled, "*down where the dead are.*"

I tried to resist but just like a few days ago when the coffee cup emptied it self out due to my wrist turning against my will, my right leg got out of bed. "No," my own inner voice screamed. I wanted to call my sweety but no sound came from my throat and slowly I rose from my bed. "*Look,*" said ol' gravel, mockingly, "just a bit more and then you will be where you belong." I walked to the hatch fighting my body and pulled it up on the ring. The stairs descended bathing in bright blue light, and the drumming swelled to a huge rumble that blew my mind and I gave up and unwillingly started to descend the stairs.

"I am dreaming," I told myself, "If I want to wake up, I'll be in bed." "Ha!" it sounded sharp and loud in my head, my demon voice was still inside me. "You know better, go ahead, wake up, if you can" it sounded raw and sneering now. In the meantime I descended step by step to the bright blue-lit vault. "This isn't real," I said aloud, "I'm in bed."

But I bumped my toe and felt the chill of the cold steps against my bare feet. A dark form without a face floated gently back and forth away from the bottom step. It was a shape as if someone was floating through the air in a monk's robe. An enormous fear made my heart pound. I was being waited for. "*I'm handing him over oh gracious lady*," came the raucous gravel voice, but there was no trace of mockery in the voice, and I almost tripped down the last step.

I knew where they wanted me to go and decided not to cooperate, but my heart started pounding wildly and I felt my nostrils open in fear, I would die with certainty, I would be crushed between powers I never would understand and I turned around and voluntarily took the first step to my workshop. Pulsing blue light came out as if welding was taking place and I was the only one without goggles.

The blue was so bright that it turned almost white from time to time. I tried to slow down but the woman without a face was breathing down my neck and my muscles were cramped with fear. I knew with certainty that if I turned around, that would be my last living act and I lost the ability to think rationally because the drumming became predominant and controlled my every thought. I shuffled forward and feared that my deceased neighbor would be waiting for me again. I turned slowly to the left where my workshop door should have been and shielded my eyes from the light that was now a bombardment of brilliance. I saw the contours of a cave with the intersection where blue light radiated, like a blue Roman candle spewing its blue Bengal rays into the air. "You're late," said a voice that seemed familiar to me. Why don't you come closer? " I surrendered and stepped into the cave and walked past the intersection with my eyes shielded and had to get used to the space around me.

"You don't have the bowl of innocence with you," said my neighbor accusingly, "how can you expect favors if you don't keep promises?" How is it that you do not bring the Pilates bowl with you, everything is in phase. "The favors that are not answered," said the ghostly figure, who remained half-dusk, call up unpleasantness, you bring that down on yourself. " I saw a number of figures half protruding from the cave wall, when I looked closer I saw that they were cramped in a niche.

"Friends, shall I say, you never met," said my neighbor who had followed my gaze, "they refused to cooperate, you know who they are, don't you?" They are incorporated in the gate as a warning and as decoration. ' I saw a severely burned figure and realized that the previous owners of my house had been stored and placed as watchmen.

A fourth niche was empty. "It's reserved," chuckled my neighbor who had fallen off the ladder, "do you want to know for whom?" "I don't need to know," I shivered. "For what's left of you, when you've been pecked empty," explained my former neighbor. I wanted to get away from those nasty niches and walked on and came to the opening that overlooked the plain. "We are in phase," said the shadow, and he pointed out, "the hunting fields that are infinite and eternal," he said. I was surprised to see that since my last visit to the cave, it was now high up and had endless views. I recognized the prairie I had got lost in during my first nightmare.

What seemed to be a lake shone in the distance, and the drumming seemed to come from that direction. "If you're dead," my neighbor explained, "you can't die anymore, you can just take a step and you're down." It sounded like a temptation. "Why would I want to so," I asked in disbelief, staring deep below the cave. I estimated that we were 100 meters above groundlevel and the last thing I wanted was to try such a step. "Because your love would be shred to pieces, if not" said my neighbor, "look, you can take a step where you want and see what you want."

"Look past my hand," and he pointed to the lake. I saw a line of warriors sitting around the edge behind some canoes, and a few beat drums rhythmically. In the water I saw a dot and when I looked at the dot past the hand, I saw that it was my sweetie pulled along by a current, she waved her hands but nobody saw her or rushed to her aid. "Look," my escort encouraged me, and he moved his hand and I saw the giant snake, the sea snake that did not belong in a fresh water lake, but was there. " You know where it will go, "my neighbor laughed. *"In is in and out is out,"*but sometimes in is also out or you can go from out to in, if you know what I mean. " "No," I said, "I'm not following you at all." "We're in," said my dead neighbor, "and that's out and he pointed outside."

"We all have a task, how can the dead return from the fields or how can the living enter the fields," the neighbor shouted to me, "if the innocence does not guarantee it, that was the sacrifice, we are in phase man, I already told you that last time, we all need the symbol of innocence, at the intersection, are you a retard. What is it you do not understand. Do you want your sweety to be eaten alive every hour and do you want your bowels to be emptied and then be placed in your niche? " If you are eaten in out, it casts its shadow here with us and it throws its shadow.

All kinds of thoughts swirled through my head and I began to see a line in the madness that surrounded me. "The bowl," I asked? "Yes, moron," roared my neighbor, "it has to be placed and everything changes for you or would you rather have your love eaten by an unholy rotten snake?" A dot rushed in and became a raven and clawed in my hair and started pecking at my eyes which I shielded with my hands. I woke up screaming.

The night light above our bed turned on and my wife looked at me in shock, 'what's wrong,' she asked. "The totem," I stammered, "the raven wanted to eat my guts." "Shh, you silly boy" said my sweetheart, "it was just a dream. Look, you're with me, there's no raven here." I returned to my own world and the images that had frightened me so much faded. "The lake is evil," I said at last, "you shouldn't go in there." "What do you know about my dream," asked my love sharply. "I saw you," I said, "and I couldn't help you and they want to prop me up as a watchman." "Calm down, my love," said my sweety, "I think we should have a cup of tea and then go back to sleep."

I calmed down and got out of bed and then saw that my toe was scraped where I had bumped it and I knew that it was always in and always out unless everything is in phase and then the living could become dead and the dead alive and I knew what to do. "If it helps," said my sweetheart a little later over a cup of tea, "tell me what frightened you."

"Oh well," I said, "about Indians beating the drums and stuff like that and about a lake with a giant snake swimming towards you and I felt helpless." "Dreams of impotence," said my sweetheart, "indicate problems that are on your mind and that you may or may not be able to solve." I nodded wisely, but I knew how I would solve my problem, otherwise I would have my gut pecked out and be placed in my niche and my love would stay out and suffer forever through my fault. "The bowl," I thought, "no matter how, I got to get hold of that bowl and it'll go at the intersection and then it is all behind me."

"You know, you talked too much to Barry about Indians and stuff," said my sweety, "and then you get that, you translate what you've heard into dreams or images." I took a sip of tea and thought about it. But it had been real, my toe was scraped and the blue light had blinded me. "I think you're right," I replied, "what were you and Clarene talking about? "Also about Indians," laughed my dear, "actually about Little Bighorn, Old Rock's grandfather who often accompanied her husband as a guide."

"He's chief and shaman," she added, "the Indians believe he can travel between the realm of the dead and the living." "He's working on a religious Powwow of sorts tomorrow to honor Old Rock and request that he won't leave the tribe." But he's dead, "I said," it wasn't a pretty sight, he was crushed under the wheel of a truck. " "Look, listen up," said my wife, "I don't know either, except that Barry will go there tomorrow to show his respect for his hunting friend." I let that sink in for a moment. "It's kind of a wake," my wife added, "and the tribesmen believe Little Bighorn has the power to enter both worlds in mind and spirit."

"You know," I said, "I'm going to ask Barry if I can go with him, I've seen the accident happen, and then I'm helping to say goodbye." "If you think you should do that, then do it," said my dear and drank her last sip of tea, ""but I am definitely not going along, I don't like that kind of thing, you know, reviving of the dead." "Thank you for the tea, I'm feeling a lot better again," I said, and my wife gave me her sweetest smile and said, "I'm going to turn in, are you coming too?" "Sure," I replied, "where else would I go," and somewhere far away I saw the niche that had been reserved for me. "*That wasn't half bad, dumbo*" spoke the gravel voice. "*Do you still believe in coincidences?'*

Barry was pleasantly surprised when I knocked at his door and asked if I could accompany him to the wake. "Come in first for a cup of coffee," he suggested, and a little while later we sat at his dining table with a mug of steaming coffee. "Look," said Barry, "a wake on the reservation is not the same as we are used to. For starters, do you know what a powwow is? " "No," I said, "I think it's some sort of a meeting ." "Hmm," said Barry, "yes and no, it depends on the circumstances."

The word "pow wow" is derived from the Narragansett word powwaw, "my neighbor explained, meaning" spiritual leader, "which makes Little Bighorn the main character today." "A pow-wow session begins with the Grand Entry," Barry continued, thoughtfully sipping coffee, "and in most cases, with a plea. The

Eagle Staff, the tribe of elders lead the Grand Entry while one of the guest drums invokes the great Spirit. " I felt a shudder on my back for a moment, I had heard plenty of drumming the last nights. "This event is sacred in nature," said my neighbor, "during the pow wows, there is no filming or photography. I don't think you will leave the pow wow alive if you think you should do it anyway and make no mistake about it, governmental laws don't count on the reservation. "

"I had no intention of filming or anything," I hastened to say, "I'm going to show respect." "So the drum or the guest drum invokes the great Spirit," I asked with a smile? "It's no laughing matter," said Barry, "after the last blow you feel the presence of the Great Spirit like breath on your neck." "You've been there," I asked, thinking about my basement. "I went to some pow wows," my neighbor agreed. "To understand the drum protocol, a drum can be thought of as a person or being," continued Barry, "and should be considered and respected as such. Drum etiquette is very important. The drum is the central symbol of pow wows and is located in the center of the pow wow itself formed in concentric circles. " Right, "I said," and is a wake always a pow wow? "

"In this case the vigil is a pow wow," said my neighbor, "it is religious in nature because Old Rock, was the grandson of Little Bighorn, the Shaman, and as chief and Shaman he Will make a supplication to the Great Spirit . " "And who beatsts the guest drum," I asked, just to say something. "The bravest warrior may do that," said Barry, "and to be clear, he is not a guest, but he summons up a guest, the Great Spirit or his representative." I took my last sip and got up, "I'm ready," I announced. "Then we'll go," suggested my neighbor, "you will find it interesting, these are experiences you will not soon forget." I just had the idea that Barry was right about that, I had to go and get my hands that bowl.

We got in my car and drove out of the village. I didn't know what to expect, but what I did see was the Raven skimming low over the car. I had to get my hands on that bowl even if it would cost my life, otherwise my life would be over anyway and I would end up in a niche with no guts, as a warning to future owners of my house. I had become convinced of the two worlds that touched at times and that the intersection was unfortunately under my house. If someone had told me something like that a few weeks ago, I would have shrugged and listened politely. "Another one," said Barry, pointing to a black shape on a road sign. "How nice," he said, "we're being escorted." I didn't like it at all and we were being controlled.

But of course I did not say that, imagine what I would have had to explain. Another Raven skimmed over our car. "Is it the same as before," I wanted to know? "No, this one was bigger," said my neighbor. "It's the totem," he said to himself, "you see that coincidence doesn't exist." "It is starting to look like that," I replied, setting cruise control at 70 miles per hour.

After driving for fifteen minutes, Barry said, "we have to turn right here, we're heading towards Cypress hills." "Tell me when," I said more cheerfully than I was. The landscape that had been flat and prairie-like began to show hills. "History slips by here differently," said my neighbor, "this tribe has 1,440 hectares and that has only been recognized by the state since 1913. They don't call it a reservation, but a nation. " "That would be a very small nation," in my opinion, "I said. "It doesn't work that way," said my neighbor, "all the Cree are connected no matter where their nations are, and so are the other tribes.

"There are 70 nations in Saskatchewan," continued Barry, "61 of whom are members of one of the nine Saskatchewan Tribe councils. The total population is about 129,000. But yes they are seperate tribes who do not want to be counted together. " That makes sense to me, "I said," I live in Spain and come here occasionally, but all residents of Spain are European, but our count is our count. " "There are five main languages between the nations of Saskatchewan," my neighbor went on unperturbed. We have Cree, Dakota, Dene (Chipewyan),

Nakota (Assniboine), and Saulteaux. " I hope you don't expect me to remember this, "I said, steering my car carefully on the road that was getting worse per minute.

In the distance a sign came up, "Welcome to Cree Nation," it read. "Now we are outside of Canada," laughed my neighbor, "our laws no longer count here. The Canadian police also have no say here and can not arrest anyone here. " The road stopped at a field full of old American cars. "Park here," suggested Barry. "We'll walk the rest." So we walked away from my car that I had parked with my nose to the exit in case I had to leave the pow wow quickly with a bowl in my hands and screaming Tomahawk throwing tribesmen behind me.

We walked up the hill and when we came down the other side we saw the huge Totem pole that watched over the village and stood in the middle of an open area. I saw it right away, on top was a Raven watching me, or at least I had that feeling. When I turned around I saw that his head had turned as well, following me. There were people in colorful robes with many beads sitting in circles around the totem pole.

A teepee had been placed under the totem pole. It was larger than ordinary wigwams and sober in color. A bare-chested man with formidable muscles walked up with a drum. "That's the guest drum," said Barry, slowly pushing his way through the crowd. "Where are we going to sit," I asked. "Next to the tent of death," replied my friend. "you mean Old Rock is in there," I asked. "Who else," said Barry. "I knew him want to be close to the body of the man who hunted with me so many times. Then I can show respect and then we'll go again. " "We're going into the tent," I asked? "After the supplication and when the Spirit is there," Barry replied as if it were the most natural thing in the world.

'He is propped up between a pair of poles, what I mean to say he's not in a coffin sort of thing," said my neighbor the Indian expert. "What do you mean he's standing up," I asked in shock. "Not much was left of him after he was smeared out," Barry explained, "so the little bit that they managed to scrape of the road has been bandaged up, like let's say, a mummy and put up, so to speak."

"Good God," I said, 'so we show respect to what has been gathered and stood up between in poles, somewhat gruesome. " "Well, it's the thought that counts," said my neighbor. "And then they'll plea," I asked, "whether the Great Spirit allows him to come back or that he at least won't leave the tribe." That's right, "said Barry," but now you have to be quiet because the drum is about to start, " and we sat down next to the tent.

The sky grew overcast and darkened. "How is it that man isn't cold," I said, pointing my head at the guest drummer. "He won't ever be cold," said Barry's, 'his upper body, has been smeared with grease, which protects against the cold and closes the pores. " "Right," I replied, amazed at everything my neighbor knew about the Cree and their traditions. The sun reappeared for a moment, and a benevolent warmth flooded the crowd.

A single drum beat rang out and a dead silence ensued. A group of old men slowly walked forward toward the circles. They looked grim, the heaviness of the moment radiated from them. In the center of them was a curiously dressed figure, with bison horns and a feather collar. They stopped at the first circle. A few drums were now stirred and they moved to the second circle. The drums no longer held back but became rhythmically hypnotic in nature. A hard blow cut right through the drumming.

"That was the guest drum," my neighbor whispered, "and the man in the middle is Little Bighorn." After the beat that still thundered over the field and then ebbed away over the field, the men moved to the third circle, which was smaller in nature. "The Eagle staff," said Barry only, "doing the grand entry." The guest drum started to produce a regular thump and the man who struck it looked intensely concentrated. His eyes were closed, but his face twitched by every beat.

The Eagle staff now reached the totem pole and they sat down with their backs to it facing the crowd. The drumming of the group that had touched the lighter drums stopped, and the guest drum was now the only one to blast out loudly over the heads of those present. The strokes followed each other more and more quickly until it seemed like a continuous sound that swelled and ebbed away. I understood what Barry had meant by explaining that a drum had a soul that could be raised. Little Bighorn got up from the Totem pole and pointed to the sun, screaming with outstretched hand something I didn't understand. The guest drum was now beaten like crazy and the lighter drums were gently touched.

Little Bighorn had become the mediator, he looked up wildly and took a few steps forward. I watched him enchanted. He looked down at the floor and bent down and in one swift movement he took a handful of sand and threw it up. The drums were silent now. The mediator spread his arms upwards and let out a screeching scream at the cloudy sky, stamping on the ground. The guest drum gave a blow. Little Bighorn lifted his left foot and touched the earth with his right hand and screamed and I knew it were not words but a primal sound that came from his heart and invoked a multitude of powers.

He was becoming one with his environment. He bellowed out his lungs and the guest drum was beaten like crazy and slowly the medicine man rose and started leaping about. The warrior who mistreated the drum looked like if hewas in a trance, the sweat was running down his face over his shoulders, his arms and glistening on his chest. The circles swayed to the beat and it was a revelation to me how synchronized it went, were Barry and I really the only ones who didn't feel the beat?

The Shaman's eyes were turned upward, and as he moved past us in an intricate dance. I only saw the whites of his eyes, he was turned inwardly and was fulfilling the role of mediator between the tribe and the Great Spirit. The Eagle staff started to make a sound between the drumbeats that sounded like oem oem oem and With every 'Oem' the rhythm became wilder and the magician flew almost past the circle of faces that looked up at him in ecstasy. Then it happened. A thunderclap in clear sky.

The air was about to be torn apart, and the smell of Ozone dominated the scene. The shaman froze in his movements and the guest drum fell silent. "The Great Spirit is among us," whispered my neighbor, "do you feel the presence?" Slowly the Shaman came back to life, holding his hands in front of him as if he were carrying something invisible and round in front of him, then bringing his hands to his heart. His hands went where his heart would have been and he slowly brought them forward again and then he raised his hands over his head. He had offered his heart to those present.

The gesture was unmistakable. He uttered a few plaintiff cries that were intensely sad, then pointed to the warrior at the guest drum who gave it a huge blow. He beckoned an old Eagle staff warrior standing next to him at the totem pole. Little Bighorn strode to the tent with stiff steps worthy and dignified and turned away the front flap. He walked in wailing and a huge feeling of uneasiness crept over me. It took a long time filled with spine-chilling screams and then there was a pleading murmur and then he emerged behind the tent and I understood that there was also a back flap, he had been wailing incantations at Old Rock.

The guest drum gave a blow and everyone bounced up. The Shaman was back. I then saw what he was holding in his hands, it was undeniably the blessing bowl. He held it over his head and circled the circle whimpering in a way that made my blood freeze. He stopped facing the guest drum, which was now beating madly, and reached into the bowl and threw a handful of ashes in every direction of the wind and wept. Tears streamed down his cheeks and I watched the raven sitting on the totem pole float down and sit at his feet. Little Bighorn nodded to the old Eaglestaff warrior, who took the bowl from him and walked around the circle, scattering ashes here and there, then approaching his chief again.

The rest was in a trance and outside of the drum beats came the addictive oem oem oem incantation. I was watching with wide-open eyes. I weighed my chances if I would jump forward and snatch the bowl then I wouldn't get out of here alive, the desecration would be total. I decided to wait for a better opportunity. The EagleStaf warrior held out the bowl and Little Bighorn took a hunting knife from his pouch and cut his left arm. The blood was collected in the bowl. He held up his arm and let out wailing cries, like you would expect from an animal in pain. It had been a deep cut, and blood was now dripping on to his feather collar.

He nodded at the warrior who turned away with the bowl and headed back toward the tent and disappeared through the front flap. Mesmerized, I watched Little Bighorn smear the blood of his left arm, over his face with his right hand and cry and wail as the drum drove people mad. Suddenly he called out something and the tribesmen rose to their feet and made careful dance steps with the totem pole in the middle. Barry also got up and joined me and I saw my chance when I saw the old warrior coming from behind the tent. I left everyone behind, and carefully exited the circle towards the tent and once I got there I danced towards the back. The guest drum was now deafening and my heart was pounding but I knew what to do.

I looked over my shoulder one last time and saw the heaving and dancing circles as if in a trance, half stooping and then straightening up again, accompanied by a drum that drowned out every thought. The back flap moved gently in the light wind that had blown up and to the left and right of the opening the laces, which were intended to close it, moved gently back and forth. With one quick step, I was in the teepee. I saw the two torches on either side of the uptight and indeed bandaged body. On the floor in front of Old Rock where he only rested with one leg on the ground, my bowl was resting on a furry skin. "It's mine," I thought with a sense of joy, who would have thought I'd ever be happy to see that damned bowl?

What to do, would I put it under my shirt or just walk out the back flap with the bowl in my hands and go over the hill to my car. "Barry?" That thought came up a bit guiltily. "Every man for himself," I thought, after all it was about my love who would be devoured by a serpent, and my guts that would be torn from my body and my remains that would guard the gate forever in a niche. I bent down without even giving the mummy as much as a glance. I turned the bowl upside down to let the ash whirl out and was just ready to sneak off when the front flap opened.

I jumped up in panic, bowl in my hand, and my foot hooked behind a cable that ran down the pole to keep Old Rock up. "**Ugh,**" I heard behind me. I tore my foot loose and I shouldn't have, because now the mummy fell forward on the torches and I don't know what was under the bandages, but it caught fire immediately. The great warrior looked at me with wide eyes and then jumped forward. With a catlike jump, I went through the back flap and without wanting to, I kicked the main teepee stick over. I watched the skins catch fire as the wigwam collapsed and I should have helped the Native American warrior but I would have been the last to set the bowl down. "Everyone for themselves," I thought for the second time in a few minutes. "He shouldn't have come in, anyway." I sprinted up the hill and stopped halfway, breathless with a blood taste in my throat from running. I looked back and saw Little Bighorn pointing in my direction and I ran up the last few meters and saw my loyal Chrysler. The roof was black with ravens nesting on it. "I got it," I called from afar, "get out of here," I screamed, "look you bloody ravens," and running to the car, I held up the bowl.

I heard noises from horses behind me and knew there was nothing to do but try to escape, raven or not, my car was the only rescue. The ravens took off and flew over me in a cloud and I reached the car and put the bowl on the roof. I frantically searched for my keys in my pockets and then felt them in my bodywarmer. I pressed the button and the doors unlocked. I saw how the ravens flew at the Indians and started pecking at themas if they were a sweet treat. Two fell off their horses trying to rip the ravens off their heads with both hands. I started the car and luckily it started immediately, I tapped the shift in drive and stopped, the bowl was still on the roof!

I jumped out and snatched the blasted thing from the roof and dove back into the car. I put the car in drive and with spinning tires and throwing up dust I tore away. It was just in time, I threw a sandstorm up behind me and saw a cloud of smoke rising above the dust. "That will be Old Rock's Teepee," I thought, "and maybe some neighboring wigwams, boy, that is not how to make friends." I reached the asphalt and immediately accelerated, the American jumped sharply to the left and was then under control and a little later the big V8 groaned under the torture of maximum rpm on the main road. I looked in my mirror and saw five dots coming from the dirt road. "They are coming for me," I knew with certainty, "and if they overtake me, they will kill me. It's not every day that a stranger sets a dead brave on fire during a Pow wow. "

I noticed the railway barriers were going down as I approached my village. I squirted underneath. "Welcome," the sign read. "*Where the past is the present.*" I réally understood the meaning now under the village code of arms. Everything was in a muddle, past or present and Indians were after me and I had a bowl next to me that had only caused misery in my life and that had to be in the basement at an intersection to open up dimensions.

I drove uncontrollably fast into my street and stopped in front of my house. I didn't even turn the engine off. I grabbed the bowl of the passenger seat and ran to the front door. I banged hard on the door in pure panic as the first cars entered the street. "Bloody barriers were open again," I thought. My love opened the door, "What is the matter," she asked? "Lock the door behind me," I shrieked, and ran as fast as my legs allowed me to, into the bedroom. I went full speed towards the hatch and pulled it up on the ring and the blue light shone everywhere. "We're in phase," was my only thought as I dashed down the stairs into the basement. Upstairs I heard a banging and kicking at the door.

The drumming started at the last step. It banished every thought, I had no time for that either, above me a tribe of wild warriors was trying to kick my door in. I jumped to my workplace in leaps and bounds. My dead neighbor half stepped out to meet me, "Hurry up," he called out, time is limited. " Get out of my way, "I shouted, pushing him roughly aside. The light was dazzling, but it was not difficult to find the spot that was brightest. On my knees I crawled forward and placed the bowl on it with a firm motion.

It was almost blown out of my hands. "Other way around, you retard," the rough gravel voice cussed at me in my head. I responded and turned the bowl half a turn and felt it sink somewhat like a key in a keyhole. A huge thud sounded and the air was torn as if a bolt of lightning exploded under my hands. I was lifted off my feet and shot through space like a toy doll. I flew like a cork from a champagne bottle at a dizzying speed past the dead guards. I had just enough consciousness to look at the lake past my hand. I skimmed over the prairie and the light changed its intensity several times around me.

"ha," was my first thought, "I'm a meteorite." The drumming Indians rushed closer and I saw the lake and then my speed dropped and I fell from the sky, next to the canoes. I saw my sweetheart in the lake and I saw the twisting movement swimming towards her. I hadn't had time to aim when I had looked past my hand and like a failing superman I had fallen out of the blue in the wrong place.

"A Canoe, my kingdom for a canoe," I thought, and I jumped into the nearest canoe that had a paddle and pushed off. "Ugh," I heard indignantly, and thinking while paddling like a madman, I thought "it's not exactly my Indian day." My love was now treading water and saw me rushing towards her and was screaming at the top of her lungs but all my strength and attention was in the paddle that I made bite into the water faster and faster.

At full speed I passed the shape that swam towards my wife and reached her a few canoe lengths before the serpent that was now sticking its head out of the water. "Hang over the canoe quickly," I called. " The slender boat almost turned over and with all my strength I counterbalanced and then my love lay across the width of the slender vehicle. "Closer to me," I roared when I saw the tip threatening to submerge, and I hung as far back as I could.

My dear did just that and she shuffled a little closer to me and after that she dared not move anymore, because every movement threatened to overturn the vessel. I started paddling like crazy again and saw the island getting closer .. We had become top heavy but went about as fast as the serpent that followed us. Even when the keel hit the ground, I was still paddling. My sweety jumped up and ran, splashing the water up high, onto the beach and I was still paddling.

A stroke almost overturned my boat and the serpent was there and I smacked it on its ugly head with all my strength and jumped out of the boat. I waded backwards to the beach as fast as I could. My feet protested the sharp stones trying to drill into the soles of my feet, but I kept my eye on the mouth that looked at me lurking and could rush forward any moment to drag me away back to the deep. I held the paddle half-raised like a melee weapon. Then the water was around my calves and I turned around and ran for my life and kept running even when I was already plowing through the hot sand.

When I turned around I saw that I was about 20 meters from the waterline and the movement that stirred the water was the serpent making its way back to deeper parts of the lake. "Thank you," said my sweetheart, "that was just in time." "You can say that again," I replied, "I could not have come any later." "How did you get into my dream," she asked. "This is dream time, I guess," I replied, "or the eternal hunting grounds or whatever you want to call it, and I will always help you, you know that." "Silly boy," she said, then added, "I know, I wouldn't expect anything else." "Is this reality," she asked, "or is this a place where we meet before we wake up." "***There is no reality***," I said, putting my arms around her, "we are real and the rest is nonsense, ***reality is what you make of it.***"

"That really is the way it is, huh," she laughed. "You betcha," I replied, "that's forever and ever." If we want to wake up, we'll have to go there, "I said, pointing to the cave opening where bright blue light broke out. "Hmm," she said, "I don't know if I would like to, it's beautiful here. And if this is the hereafter, *then we are two souls who have found each other.* " *"I found you years ago,"* I smiled, *"and it's the best thing that ever happened to me."* I still had my eyes on the cave and saw how slowly the blue glow got less and less bright and eventually disappeared. "I think we have gone out of phase," I said, "let's make the most of it, and a sense of happiness filled me such as I had rarely experienced as a partial aspect of my life.

"Did you sleep well, I asked my love," when she came out of the bedroom. "Yes," she replied with a beaming smile, "would you like some coffee?" "I think that would be very nice," I said, watching her click the machine on and press the double expresso button for me. "It was a nice dream," she continued, "we were on an island, a beautiful tropical island, and we were very happy." I am always happy with you, "I laughed and meant it.

"I like tropical areas," I said, and picked up the morning newspaper. "We also traveled about a lake in a canoe or something," said my sweety, "but you know how it is, dreams blur away once you are awake and one only remembers shreds." "Dreams are deceptional," I said just to say something. "That's what people without dreams say," my sweetheart laughed. I thought that was very profound in the early morning, but there was something to be said for it. After the second cup of coffee I put the newspaper away. "You know," I started, "it's nice to be here,

I'm happy with you here, far away from Europe, away from the hustle and the bustle." She looked at me and smiled. "It's jet lag," I said, "which always affects me for a few days, but then I become Canadian again, and if it wasn't for our kids or grandchildren, I would never go back." "I know what you mean," she replied seriously. "I'm a different person here, too, and I'm genuinely happy here. Here we live in a different reality. " "Reality is just an agreement," I said, "it's just what you make of it and when you realize that, you have to make sure that your happiness is in that reality or you have to look further, because time is something that never returns. " "It's different here," my wife laughed, "you know, where the past is the present." "It's a cowboy village," I agreed, "people are more down to earth here, they realice

there is no past or present, but both are intertwined and form a happy mix with daily life." "But you do look a bit pale," said the love of my life. "Why don't you go around the block and get a bit of a breath, it will do you good." 'My cup tinkled on my saucer, a heavy lumber truck, had passed by and the streets had not been made for that in 1901. The large, freshly cut logs protruded from the trunk and a red cloth fluttered at the end. "They are driving way too fast," my wife thought, "how should something like that ever make an emergency stop?" I took my last sip of coffee and put my cup back on the saucer and got up to put it on the counter. "

"Thanks for the coffee," I said, "I will go for a walk about, I might go past the Thriftstore of the Salvation Army, sometimes you come across nice second-hand things and you always help charity a bit.' "I'll see you later," said my sweetie, and she poured herself some more coffee. The wind was blowing and my ears and nose got cold. "Stands to reason," I thought, "they do stick out a bit." Like a turtle I pulled my neck back in a little and walked to the end of the street. At the Ford Dealer's parking lot, I briefly looked at prices that were on F 150s.

They did look cool, 1/2 ton trucks with a double cabin and a large loading platform. You saw half the village driving around in them. "Good God," I thought, "they started new at $ 80,000, and with luck you could buy yourself a house for that." I turned the corner towards 'Thriftstore' and saw an Indian man coming out with a package under his arm. I saw an old American gas guzzler pull over at the curb and the window rolled down and the Indian handed over the package to the driver that took it from him. I was almost behind him now and started for the Thiftstore, I held back a moment and looked in the shop window to see if there was something in there to my liking.

The Indian man looked to the right and stepped on the road to cross. He should have looked left and right, of course, and out of nowhere a lumbertuck appeared, honking loudly with the hiss of the air brake on full, racing down at the poor devil. I jumped forward and roughly pulled the man back, the poor fellow looked at the truck as if frozen. The 40 tonner swizzed by, just missing the Indian's moccasins. "Man," I said, "that was a close shave." The man seemed to be nailed down, then unfroze. "I really didn't see him," he stammered.

"I understand that," I said, "they are driving way too fast and are top-heavy and appear out of the nowhere." A motorcycle stopped next to us, "Man, Old Rock," said the helmeted figure, "I thought you were a goner. **Ugh**, that was almost the hunting grounds for you." He took off his helmet and I saw that he looked very shocked indeed. Less from the Thriftstore came out, "man," he said, "that was almost a direct hit, the Lord has kept you in his hand. The man addressed as Old Rock now started trembling all over. "I just made some tea,"

Les continued, "you boys want to come in and have some?" I think that's a good idea, said the Indian with the motor bike and he put it on the stand. "I came to pick him up," he said, pointing his head at Old Rock. "It was almost unnecessary." "Come on then," I replied, tea never hurt anyone. I followed the men to the door and took a last look at the shop window and saw what seemed to be a delusion in the sunlight reflected in the large window. Two figures on a tropical beach that waved at me for a moment and then I entered the Thriftstore.

San Daniel 2021

I want to thank the readers for reading and for the well-meant comments of the Tallsay writers control group .. I am always grateful if my fellow writers can relate to my story .. and now the story is finished and it is with a feeling of melancholy that I take distance.

It is done, it is finished and you all know what that means. A story must have speed and persuasion and if a story is milked out, it will lose both. I am still in doubt whether I will let it be published or let it go straight into the world, in Ebook format, but those are side issues. The story has been told, Maple Creek is a great place, with great down to Earth people and **my love** and **I** are always very happy there and now a last bit of advice from me to all of you, don't accept blessing bowls and stay healthy.. God Bless.

San Daniel

About the Author

San Daniel is an Andalusian vintner who left the academic life behind years ago. He now lives in Southern Spain. He walked into a Spanish village and never left it again. The village recognized him as a prodigal son and locked him in her arms in a warm and lasting embrace. San Daniel broke with his former life and became happy and became a vintner and writer. His heart has become Andalucian!

www.ingramcontent.com/pod-product-compliance
Lightning Source LLC
Chambersburg PA
CBHW051221160726
47994CB00002B/691